T. S. (Timothy Shay) Arthur

Hidden Wings and other Stories

T. S. (Timothy Shay) Arthur

Hidden Wings and other Stories

ISBN/EAN: 9783744750196

Printed in Europe, USA, Canada, Australia, Japan

Cover: Foto ©Andreas Hilbeck / pixelio.de

More available books at **www.hansebooks.com**

HIDDEN WINGS

AND

OTHER STORIES.

BY T. S. ARTHUR.

NEW YORK:

SHELDON & COMPANY,

335 BROADWAY (COR. OF WORTH ST.)

1864.

LIST OF SERIES.

CONTENTS.

8 CONTENTS.

"What a horrid object!"

HIDDEN WINGS,

AND OTHER STORIES.

I.

HIDDEN WINGS.

"Ugh!" said Aunt Lucy, stepping back a pace or two, and drawing her garments aside, while an expression of disgust came over her face; "what a horrid object!"

The object which had so excited Aunt Lucy was a little girl, about six years old, whom Margaret, our cook, had found sitting in the area. She was leading her in by the hand.

I turned, at Aunt Lucy's exclamation, and saw the child. She was, certainly, not beautiful; very far from it, actually repulsive. Her clothes were ragged and dirty, her feet bare, and covered with mud. Her face might have been washed within a month, but that was rather doubtful. As for her hair, the time of its last acquaintance with a comb might be set down as entirely problematical. Yes, the child was repulsive in every way.

"What on earth did you bring that creature in here for?" inquired Aunt Lucy, speaking to Margaret.

"She is a poor lone little body," replied the cook, in a sympathetic way, "wet and hungry, and I thought I'd just give her a bite, and let her warm herself. Nobody'll be any the worse for it, I'm sure."

I felt the force of Margaret's closing remark, and said—

"True enough, nobody'll be the worse off for an act of kindness. Let her sit down and dry her wet clothes, and if she's hungry, give her something to eat."

The little thing looked at me gratefully, and shrunk towards the fire. It was June, but a northeasterly storm had been blowing for the past two days. The sky was full of rain, and the air chilly as November.

Feeling certain that the poor child would

be well cared for by my kind-hearted cook, I left the kitchen, accompanied by Aunt Lucy.

"A very imp of ugliness!" exclaimed Aunt Lucy, as we entered our pleasant sitting-room, the walls of which were hung with pictures, the mantel ornamented with rich vases, while objects of taste and luxury crowded the apartment. One of these was an exquisite statuette, representing a child asleep among flowers. Certainly, nothing could have been in stronger contrast than the kitchen we had just left, with the living child there, and our elegant sitting-room, with this sculptured form of innocence and beauty.

"Only the outside, Aunt Lucy," said I; "the hard, coarse, unlovely husk. There are germs of beauty beneath all that."

"Beauty! Pah!"

Aunt Lucy's face was not very charming as she said this. The beauty of her soul was veiled for the moment.

I tried to talk with her about the innocence of childhood.

"Unlovely as that poor creature is in your

eyes," said I, "there are beneath the surface, hidden away from your view and mine, the elements of which angelic life is formed. There is a human soul there ; wonderful and mysterious thing, with its almost infinite amount of capabilities !"

"Oh, dear !" exclaimed Aunt Lucy, "don't get away off there out of my reach, with your infinite capabilities, and all that. It takes you to see angels in dirty beggar-girls. But my eyes were never so sharp-sighted."

"There may be things in heaven and earth not dreamed of in your philosophy," said I.

"I shouldn't wonder," replied Aunt Lucy, in a half-amused half-vexed manner. "I'd be a very wise woman if that wasn't so. I don't pretend to know much about what I can't see. Eyes are very convenient things, and I reckon I've got a pair sharp enough for all practical purposes. Seeing is believing."

I gave Aunt Lucy a pleasant smile and left the room, feeling interest enough in the "horrid object," as my relative had called the beggar-girl in the kitchen. Descending to Margaret's domain, I found the child sitting before the fire, a large slice of bread in her hand, which she was eating with the keen relish of hunger.

"Where do you live?" I asked, in a kind voice.

"I don't live nowhere, now," was replied, in a tone that touched my feelings.

"Don't live anywhere!" my voice expressed surprise. "How is that?"

"I lived with old Mrs. Kline before sister died, but she says I shan't stay there any longer."

"Where is your mother?"

"I haven't got any mother," she answered, lifting her eyes to mine. There was a low quiver in her voice, falling almost to a sob, as she uttered the word "mother." My interest was increasing.

"No mother?" I looked at her with pity in my heart.

"No ma'am," was her simple reply.

"Your mother is dead?"

"Yes, ma'am. She died a great while ago, when I was only a little baby. Mrs. Kline took sister and me. Jane worked for her until she got sick; then Mrs. Kline was cross, and said she'd send her to the poor-house. But she didn't, and sister died."

The child sobbed again, and tears ran over her soiled and homely face.

"When did your sister die?" I asked.

"Last week, ma'am."

"And Mrs. Kline won't let you live with her any longer?"

"No, ma'am."

"When did she send you away?"

"She sent me away yesterday."

"Yesterday! And where have you been since yesterday?"

"A woman let me sleep on the floor last night, but said I mustn't come there any more; if I did she'd send me to the station-house."

"Poor thing!" said I, pityingly, speaking to myself. "This is indeed a cruel lot for one of such tender years. What hope is

there for a child thus abandoned—thus thrust
out and left to the mercies of a hard and selfish world?"

I believed the little one's story. Though
unlovely in aspect; in fact, dirty and repulsive to the sight, there was truth in her tone
and manner. She was not deceiving me. I
had a duty to perform, and saw it clearly.
God's providence is over all his children,
the humblest, the poorest, the meanest; not
even a sparrow falls unnoticed to the ground.
I felt that he had laid upon me the duty of
caring for this little one, whose soul was as
precious in His eyes as the soul of one of my
own dear children. The case was plain. I
could not shut my eyes and turn away, and
yet be innocent.

"What are you going to do?" I asked,
again speaking to the child. I wished to see
what was in her thoughts, if, indeed, she had
any thought about the future.

"I don't know, ma'am," she answered,
with a perplexed look. "I suppose I'll have
to beg."

"Haven't you any better clothes than these?"

"No ma'am," she replied, looking down at her miserable garments.

I stood musing for a little while, turning over in my thoughts what was best to be done. The decision was soon made.

"Margaret," said I, "take her up to the bath-room and wash her thoroughly. I will find something better for her to put on; and Margaret," I added, as I was leaving the kitchen, "I think you had better cut that hair off pretty close."

Margaret said "yes ma'am," with a hearty good-will, that showed her feelings to be as much interested as mine. So I left the kitchen and went up stairs to look through my drawer for some suitable garments to replace the filthy rags I had directed to have removed. I found what I required, and leaving them in the bath-room returned to Aunt Lucy.

Now my relative was something of a character in her way. A very literalist in her modes of interpreting the common events and common aspects of life. She usually judged of people as she saw them on the outside. "It's no use," she would often say, "to be worrying yourself about what's in people, if they don't choose to talk it out and let you see what they think and feel. Show me what they do, and I'll get at their quality, fast enough."

All this was very sensible, of course, but it meant less as uttered by Aunt Lucy than if it had been said by some other person. She thought herself very shrewd and sharp, while I thought her shrewdness and sharpness often led her to forget the dictates of humanity. But she had her good points, and among these was a scorn of deceit and pretension.

"I've done many good deeds in my time," was one of her common remarks, "and have helped lots of people in distress ; put faith in beggars through the whole range of halt, lame, and blind, and came out cheated in the end. There is no virtue in the tribe. When a man, woman, or child sets up to live on alms, that moment he or she ceases to be truly honest. There is only one fair way to make a living in this world, and that is to labor for it; your vagrants should be sent to the work-house."

"Where have you been?" said Aunt Lucy, as I came into the sitting-room. She looked on me sharply and curiously; at the same time there was a little dropping of the under lip, and the appearance of an amused smile lurking about the corners of her mouth.

"In the kitchen," I replied, trying to retain the gravity of my countenance, for I saw what was in her thoughts.

"Looking after that inward beauty you talked about a little while ago?" "Aunt Lucy glanced at me quizzically.

"Margaret is washing off the dirt," I replied, laughing; "after a while I will go and see what she has found beneath. The fair, pure skin of a tender child, I guess."

"Now, you do beat all," exclaimed Aunt Lucy. "You don't say that Margaret's got that little wretch in the bath-tub?"

"Yes."

"Well, go your way, child! you'll be wiser one of these days. I suppose you intend dressing her up?"

"I shall try to make her decent and comfortable," said I.

"And how long do you suppose she'll keep so?" demanded Aunt Lucy; "I can tell you."

"How long?" I asked.

"About thirty minutes after she leaves your door; not a fraction of time longer."

"I don't understand you."

"Don't you? Then I will enlighten you a little. They'll strip the clothes from her the moment she gets home, and send her out in dirty rags again."

I smiled to myself, but did not answer.

"You don't believe it?"

"No," I answered quietly.

"Well, please goodness! but you are credulous. I know the habits of these creatures better than all that."

I did not reply, but sat turning over in my

mind the ways and means of rescuing this un-
fortunate child from the life of vagrancy to
which she had seemed destined. There was
an Asylum for orphan children in the neighborhood. I had passed it often, but never
gave the institution any special thought.
Now it assumed a just importance in my
eyes. I determined to make a visit there this
very day, and see upon what conditions its
inmates were received.

In about half an hour Margaret came in
with the metamorphosed child.

"Who is that?" asked Aunt Lucy, not re-
cognizing, on the moment, the beggar girl she
had been denouncing.

"What is your name?" I asked, taking
the little one by the hand, and looking
with rekindling interest into her homely
face.

"Ellen," she replied.

"You saw her down stairs a little while
ago," and I looked at Aunt Lucy.

"Oh! ah!"

My relation seemed a little bewildered.

"Take her down to the kitchen. I will be down after a while."

Margaret left the room.

"Wonderfully improved!" My aunt did not speak as if she were wonderfully pleased. "But, oh, dear! you can't make any thing out of them. There's an old fable about washing a pig. They put on any quantity of soap and water, but it would not wash out the swine nature. The pig was a pig still, and took kindly, after its release, to the next mud-puddle. So it will be with your protégée. That impish little face tells the whole story."

"There is a human soul there," said I, seriously; "and the soul of a child is always beautiful. The face may be unlovely, the form ungainly, and the whole outward appearance repulsive. But hidden beneath all this are forms of exquisite grace and germs of the highest excellence."

But Aunt Lucy had no patience with me.

"Talk—all talk," she replied, "and waste words with me."

So I changed the subject to one on which we were likely to have no disagreement.

In the afternoon, the storm having cleared away, I dressed myself to go out, and made a visit to the Orphan Asylum. I was pleased with every thing I saw there, and more pleased at being able to gain admission for the child, whose destitute condition had awakened my interest.

About a week after this time Aunt Lucy and I were sitting near an open window, through which the soft, warm air of a bright summer day was pressing. Suddenly my aunt started, with an expression of shuddering disgust on her countenance, and pointing to the skirt of her dress, exclaimed :

"Ugh! just look at that horrid thing! knock it off!"

I glanced down and saw a caterpillar. Aunt Lucy was quite excited about the harmless little creature ; but I stooped, and holding my handkerchief close to her dress, gently removed it. As I rose up, I said, still looking at the unsightly animal,

"There is not much beauty here, certainly."

"Throw it out of the window!" exclaimed Aunt Lucy, her face still expressing strong disgust.

But I held the now motionless creature close to my eyes, and examined it curiously. It was nearly black, with rough protuberances all over the body. These were surmounted by thorny looking hairs, which gave it a spiteful and venomous aspect. If I had not been looking deeper than the surface I should have felt as great a repugnance to the animal as did Aunt Lucy. But I saw more than the simple larva.

"Why don't you throw it out of the window? It will bite or poison you!"

"No danger of that," I returned; "if not handsome, it is at least harmless, and carries in its bosom a world of beauty."

And saying this, I stepped into the garden, and plucking a few poplar leaves, brought them in and laid them upon the window-sill. Placing the caterpillar upon one of them, it commenced eating immediately, cutting away the tender pulp, and leaving bare the thread-like fibres.

"See here, Aunt Lucy," said I, "isn't this curious?"

"What?" and she came and stood looking over my shoulder. "What is curious?" she repeated.

"Just see how eagerly it devours that leaf."

"Humph! I don't see any thing so strange in a caterpillar eating," replied my aunt, in a contemptuous way. "You can see that going on by the wholesale out in the garden, at any time. Do kill the hateful thing!"

"No," said I, a new thought coming into my mind. "I'm going to watch its trans-formation."

"Its what?"

"Its change from ugliness to beauty;" and taking up the leaf upon which it was feeding, I carried it carefully from the room and up to my chamber, where I placed it in an open box. For two or three days I kept the greedy thing supplied with leaves, the soft portions of which it removed in the most perfect manner, leaving delicate fibrous skeletons—curious relics of its destructive work. On the third day it became sluggish and refused to eat. I then placed it in a small box perforated with holes to admit air, and left it to undergo that most wonderful of all changes which animated nature presents. On examining the box a few days afterward I found that my caterpillar had disappeared, but in its place was a compact silky mass. I could not but look upon this with feelings of astonishment and admiration. What strange instinct! what singular skill! The animal had woven for itself a winding-sheet of exquisite fineness.

I did not show my cocoon to Aunt Lucy. I wanted to surprise her with something more—I wished to reveal to her the hidden wings, star-gemmed and rainbow-hued, which had been folded up in the body of that repulsive worm, the life of which she had asked me to crush out. There was a lesson in all this for me—a lesson for her also, if she would only read it. My hope was that the page would exhibit lucid truth for her eyes.

Daily I examined my chrysalis for signs of the new birth. This was continued for more than a week, when, one morning, in lifting the edge of the lid carefully, I saw the glitter of painted wings. Without unclosing the box I carried it down to the sitting-room.

"I have something to show you, Aunt Lucy," said I, my face all aglow with pleasure.

"What is it?" she asked; "a new bracelet from your extravagant husband?"

"Something more beautiful and more wonderful than any bracelet ever formed by the hand of man," I replied.

"Well, what is it? Don't mystify me."

"I don't mean to. You remember the ugly caterpillar I took from your dress a week or two ago? Here it is," and I uncovered my box, when out flew a butterfly. Sailing gracefully across the room, it alighted on a heliotrope that was blooming in the window, and sat there gently fanning its delicate wings, which were of a dark purplish color, dotted with blue spots and surrounded with a bright yellow border.

Aunt Lucy struck her hands together and exclaimed, "What a beauty! Why, it's a mourning-cloak!" and she moved across the room and stood looking at the insect admiringly.

"If I had killed the caterpillar you would never have seen this butterfly."

She turned, and looked at me inquiringly.

"Caterpillar! I don't understand you?"

"I told you there was beauty hidden in the repulsive creature,—delicate wings of exquisite texture and color folded up in that writhing little body."

"There now, child, do talk in plain common sense language! What do you mean?"

"Simply and plainly, that the worm I brushed from your dress was the larva of this mourning-cloak. I fed the caterpillar on poplar leaves until it was ready for its change, then laid it in this box to spin its cocoon. You see here the silken envelope through which the insect has cut its way."

Aunt Lucy was taken by surprise. I improved the opportunity to say:

"There is a lesson for us here. We must not judge too hastily from what lies merely on the surface, whether of things or persons. There is an inner as well as an outer life; the unseen as well as the visible; and it is not always that the visible gives to common sight a true representation of the invisible. There are rudiments of a higher life than first manifests itself in every individual that is born. If there is so much loveliness hidden in a caterpillar, what may we not look for in a human soul? Two weeks ago there was a greedy, destructive worm, that fed itself on coarse bitter leaves with an insatiable appetite; but now it has been transformed into an airy being that floats on the lightest zephyr, and sips honeyed nectar from flower-cups more exquisitely painted than china of Sévres."

I paused, and my aunt looked at me with the air of one in slight bewilderment.

"Two weeks ago," I continued, "a dirty little beggar-girl, repulsive enough to look upon, came to our door. I think you felt toward her very much as you felt toward the worm. You manifested the same disgust at her foul and unsightly aspect. I suggested that there might be something beneath the surface more attractive than met the eyes. But you saw only a vagrant, on whom all kindness would be thrown away. I felt differently and thought differently. I looked below the surface and saw hidden wings, destined, it might be, to unfold in spiritual atmospheres."

"I hope it may all come out so," replied Aunt Lucy, with something subdued in her manner; "but if you find any wings about that creature you will make a wonderful discovery. She isn't the kind."

"Time will show," said I, as I pushed open the window and let my little prisoner float out into the garden.

Time passed on, and my good aunt, who
was not much wiser for the lesson I had endeavored to teach her, continued to judge
of things in her old way. She did not forget
the caterpillar and butterfly, however, nor
my homely little protégé of the dirty face and
ragged garments, slyly asking me now and
then if I saw any signs of the "hidden
wings." I must confess that after I had
gained admission for the child in the Orphan
Asylum, my interest for her abated. I had
done all that common charity required me to
do for the little outcast, and it is not surprising that the absorbing cares and duties of
my home caused me to forget her almost entirely.

Aunt Lucy, who was my mother's sister, a
spinster, and past the age of fifty, did not
mellow and sweeten with advancing years.
There were asperities in her character which
the attrition of life failed to remove. Loneli-
ness and some hard experiences had tended
to narrow her thoughts into a small circle,
. and she grew more selfish and less kindly in

her feelings toward others as she grew older. Her presence often threw discord into our family circle, and I had frequently to come between her and other members of our household, and soothe with kind words the feelings she had jarred.

It is ten years from that wet June day on which our story opens. Aunt Lucy is sick—hopelessly bed-ridden, and requiring almost constant attention. I had tried my best to make her comfortable, to win her thoughts away from herself, to inspire her with patience, to throw into her gloomy and complaining mind some rays of sunshine; but I failed utterly. She was peevish, dissatisfied, and always imagining herself neglected. The truth was, she had so little about her that was attractive, and so much of the repellent, that no one went to her room except in obedience to the voice of duty. At last my husband insisted upon our procuring a nurse, whose sole business should be to attend upon the invalid. A middle-aged woman was obtained, but Aunt Lucy quarrelled with her, and she threw up the situation in less than a week.   Then another was found, but the result was the same; a third, and she left in three days.   I was in despair.

Thus it was, when one day a plainly dress-ed girl between sixteen and seventeen years of age entered my sitting-room.

"You don't know me," she said, seeing I looked at her strangely.

"I do not," was my answer.

"My name is Ellen."

"Ellen? Ellen?" I said in an inquiring tone.   The girl was a stranger to me.   I had no recollection of ever having seen her.

"Don't you remember," she said, "the poor little girl you were kind to many years ago? I have been in the Asylum ever since."

I looked at her in surprise.   I had scarcely thought of her for years.

"Are you that poor forsaken little child?"

"I was, ma'am," she answered, with a tre-mor in her voice; "but, thanks to your good-ness, I am something better now.   I must leave the Asylum, but I could not go without seeing you and telling you of the gratitude that is in my heart. I pray for you every day, ma'am, and ask God to bless you for your kindness to a friendless orphan."

I was deeply touched by this unexpected visit and acknowledgment. I arose, and taking her hand, looked into her plain, unattractive face, that was all alive with feeling, and said:

"And this is Ellen? Your thanks and gratitude are more than a double reward for that one act of kindness that cost me so little. And you are going to leave the Asylum?"

"Yes, ma'am; as soon as I can find a place."

"What do you intend doing?" I asked.

"I should like to get a place as chambermaid, or to do plain sewing."

I thought of Aunt Lucy, pushed the thought from my mind—thought of her again, and said:

"Could you undertake to nurse an old lady who is sick?"

3

"I am too young and inexperienced for that," she replied.

I looked down and mused for some time. It hardly seemed right to put one so young to such hard service as an attendant on Aunt Lucy. I had the girl in my power, bound by the strong chain of gratitude, and I was not generous enough to release her. So I told her of my sick relative, and my desire to procure a nurse; asked her to take the situation and gained her consent. On the next day she was an inmate of my family.

During the first two or three days Aunt Lucy was captious, ill-natured, fretful, and difficult to please; but Ellen's patience never wearied, her feet never tired, her hands never hung down. She was kind, thoughtful, and gentle. I looked on, and now and then spoke a word of encouragement or excuse, but I found Ellen more ready even than myself with excuses for the unhappy, self-tormenting invalid.

"She is old and sick, and in pain, ma'am," Ellen would answer me, "and that is sad. I pity her too much to grow impatient. We must bear with the infirm and the suffering."

In the second week affairs in Aunt Lucy's room began to put on a new appearance. The old lady was softening—the hardness of her nature giving way. Sunshine had been around her for many days, and its warmth was penetrating the frozen surface of her heart. She complained less, was less fretful, easier to please, and had longer seasons of quiet and calmness.

One evening, in passing the door of her chamber, I heard Ellen reading aloud. The door stood slightly ajar, and I stopped to listen. Her tones were loud enough for me to hear distinctly. She was reading the twenty-third Psalm, beginning, "The Lord is my shepherd; I shall not want." Every word of that beautiful Psalm was familiar to my ear; I had heard it read a hundred times—read by the preacher and read by the child. But never did its impressive language come to my heart with such a fulness of meaning as it came now, borne on the low, tender, reverent voice of that stranger-girl.

She paused at the last verse. There was stillness for a few moments. Then I heard Aunt Lucy say, in a mild, subdued tone—so mild and subdued that I hardly recognized it—"Read on, child; it does me good."

And Ellen read on—

"The earth is the Lord's, and the fulness thereof; the world, and they that dwell therein."

She went on to the close of that chapter, when she paused again.

There was another brief period of silence, when I heard Aunt Lucy say,

"Thank you, child; that will do. I shall sleep now."

I passed on noiselessly, my heart full, and new thoughts pressing into my mind.

"The wings are unfolding," I said, "the inner beauty revealing itself. Aunt Lucy, in her blindness, would have crushed the worm which, in its transformation, now gladdens her eyes with its beauty."

Shall I go on, reader? No! the lesson is complete. Daily I observed Ellen, and saw that she was influenced by deep religious feelings; that there had been a birth of spiritual life in her soul, and that this life was putting on the outward forms of that true charity which not only suffereth long and is kind, but shows its heavenly origin in a faithful performance, from unselfish motives, of every known duty. I did not have to remind Aunt Lucy of the error she had committed; she saw it herself, and many times spoke, half sadly and half wonderingly, of the change which a few years had wrought.

"I would have spurned her once, as a thing offensive to the sight," she said to me one day, as her eyes followed Ellen from the room ; "and now she has grown into an angel, and blesses me daily with her heavenly ministrations."

II.

THE RICH MAN'S BENEFACTOR.

A POOR man, miserably clad, was trundling a wheelbarrow load of stones. The day was hot and sultry, and the sweat poured in streams down his wasted, sun-burnt face. He looked labor-worn and discontented. His load was heavy, and as the wheel jarred over the inequalities in his way, the jerkings and contortions of his body were painful to look upon.

An elegant carriage, drawn by a pair of sleek, fat horses, drove by. In it sat the rich owner of many thousands of acres. His face wore, also, a look of discontent. Different as was his lot from that of the indigent day-laborer—surrounded, as he was, by all external means of happiness, waited upon, ministered to, courted, flattered—he was, if the truth were known, no happier than the poor complainer he had swept heedlessly by.

Two men were sitting at the window of a cottage, and saw this passing phase of human life.

"Poor Jim Coyle," said one of them; "I always pity that man."

"And poor Edward Logan," said the other; "I always pity him."

"You waste your pity, then," remarked the other, whose name was Howard.

"I am not so sure of that," was replied; "in my view old Mr. Logan is more entitled to sympathy than Jim Coyle, for he is, I think, the most miserable of the two. And where there is most wretchedness there is most need of pity."

"Let him pity himself," said Howard, a little sharply, "if he stands in need of that sentiment. I'll waste none upon him. Having all the means of happiness within his reach, if he don't choose to enjoy himself, why, that's his business, not mine. There are enough of the hopelessly and helplessly wretched to look after."

" None more hopelessly and helplessly

wretched, in my view, than Edward Logan," said the other, whose name was Strong. "True, he has the means of enjoyment, in rich abundance around him, and the same may be said of Jim Coyle. Both are unhappy because they fail to use aright the God-given powers they posess."

"I should like to see the rich abundance possessed by Jim Coyle," said Howard, looking at his friend with some surprise.

"The sources of happiness are not found in the mere possession of this world's goods, else would the rich only be in felicity, while the poor would be doomed to a joyless life. The true means of delight can be had in as great abundance by the one as by the other. Your Jim Coyles may be as happy as your Edward Logans; yet each remain, as to the possession of worldly goods, in the same condition as now."

"Do you mean to say, friend Strong," said Howard, "that Jim Coyle would not be happier if his toil were made lighter, and his reward continue the same?"

"He might be, but I have my doubts. There is a class of men that, like the bee, take honey from the flowers; there is another class that, like the caterpillar, feed only on bitter leaves. I think both Jim Coyle and Edward Logan are of this latter class. They get no honey from the flowers. Place them in what circumstances you will, and they find the bitter, but not the sweet."

"Prettily enough said," answered Howard, "but not the fact, in my opinion. Observation tells me that a man's external condition has almost every thing to do with his happiness. Can a man be happy who works in pain and weariness; who is hungry, while others are fed to repletion; whose famishing children cry to him for the bread which he cannot give them; who sees his wife wasting daily under the pressure of toil and duty, which he has no power to lighten; who is oppressed, and no one takes up his cause?—I tell you, my friend, the external condition has every thing to do with a man's happiness."

"Why, then, let me ask, is not Mr. Logan happy? Could any condition be more favorable?"

"A guilty conscience, perhaps," said Howard.

"I was not aware," remarked Strong, "that there was occasion for trouble in that direction. What has he done? What crime has he committed? I never heard any great wrong charged against him. The world bears testimony that he is an honest man."

"He may be honest," was replied, "in the common acceptation of the word. But how a man, rolling in wealth, can see want and misery all around him, without relieving it, conscience clear, is more than I can understand."

"I judge no man," said Mr. Strong. "If, as to external act, he keeps the commandments inviolate, I leave his conscience with him and his God. But, as I said before, I think Mr. Logan quite as much entitled to sympathy as Jim Coyle—more so, in fact, for from habit, circumstance, and range of thought and feeling, he is capable of greater suffering. Jim Coyle's thoughts move in a very narrow circle; his wants have never grown into very large dimensions; give him idleness, and enough to eat and drink, and he will be satisfied. You cannot say this of Mr. Logan. He has every luxury the body can desire, and time enough to enjoy it. Is he happy? Look at his face!"

"I hardly have patience to hear you talk after this fashion," said the other. "Who cares whether he's happy or not, the hard-hearted, close-fisted old wretch! Don't talk to me about pitying him."

"I pity him, nevertheless, and from my heart. I never see him but I set myself to pondering his case, turning it over and over, and searching in my thoughts for some way of helping him."

"You! You help Edward Logan!" and Howard laughed heartily at the idea. "You had better elect yourself his benefactor."

"Just what I've seriously thought of doing," said Strong. "Now let me make this proposition. You pity Jim Coyle. Elect yourself his benefactor. I pity Edward Logan, and will elect myself his benefactor. Keeping our own counsel, let us see if we cannot help both of these men to enjoy life better."

Somewhat amused at this novel suggestion, Howard agreed, and the two men separated.

Mr. Strong was really in earnest. His business was that of a conveyancer and real estate agent. This brought him into frequent intercourse with Mr. Logan, and gave him opportunities for close observation. He knew the man well—his character, his means, his peculiarities, his weaknesses, and his prejudices. He loved money; it was his idol. He started in life with a small inheritance, determined to accumulate, and he had been successful. Dollar had been added to dollar, house to house, and field to field, until now, at sixty-five, he was the richest man in his neighborhood. But, as we have seen, wealth had not brought happiness; so far from it, if he was the richest man in his neighborhood, he might also be set down as the most miserable. He had one son, but, as he had loved money more than his child, the boy was neglected for gold. A neglected child is almost certain to wander from the right way, and get into the road to ruin. The feet of Mr. Logan's child went astray. He grew up self-willed, inclined to vices, and impatient of control. At twenty-one he was an idle, dissipated spendthrift. At thirty he was killed in a drunken brawl. Mr. Logan had also a daughter. But the one great pursuit of his life absorbed all his affections, and there were none left for the little blossom that opened in his household. She did not learn to love the cold, abstracted man she called her father. There was something about him that repelled her, something that prevented her from coming to his side or climbing upon his knee. He made chilly the atmosphere of his home, so that this flower did not unfold in richness and fragrance. The mother was a nervous invalid, between whom and her husband no true sympathy existed. If they had ever loved each other, their love died and was buried long before little Helen grew into conscious girlhood.

When Helen was nineteen, a not very remarkable circumstance occurred, but one which had the effect to set the mind of Mr. Logan all on fire with interest for his daughter. A young man in the neighborhood, who had nothing to recommend him but a good education, integrity of character, industry, and poverty, was bold enough to ask for the hand of Helen in marriage. Mr. Logan said "No," in anger and insult. Things turned out as they usually do in such cases, and the young lovers took the responsibility of getting married. The feet of Helen, since that time, had never recrossed the threshold of her father's house, and though ten long years had intervened, she had known more of true happiness during that period than had ever come to her heart before. The neat little cottage, where she lived with her husband and children, stood not very far away from her father's imposing mansion, and if the old man did not look upon it daily, it was because he turned his eyes resolutely away. Long ago the daughter had ceased to make any overtures to her father. All that she could do to break down the hard wall of separation, she had done. But he refused to be reconciled. For a time he sternly forbade all intercourse between the mother and daughter; but the former set, at last, his interdict at defiance, and now few days passed in which her heart did not grow warm in the sunny home of her child.

The husband of Helen was principal in our academy, and highly esteemed by all who knew him. He was a true good man; but as he did not possess the talent of money-making, he was of no account in the eyes of Mr. Logan.

Thus it was with the richest man in the neighborhood; and Mr. Strong was right when he said he was the unhappiest. On the day following that on which our story opens, the conveyancer called over at Elm Grove, the name of Mr. Logan's beautiful place.

He was really in earnest in his desire to throw some gleams of sunshine on the rich man's shadowed way. He had often thought of his case, and often pitied him. The conversation with Mr. Howard stimulated his thought into a purpose, and now he had called to observe Mr. Logan a little more closely, and see if there was any way to lead him out of himself, for he knew that it was because he was immersed in self, that life, as to all enjoyment, had proved a failure. He found Mr. Logan sitting in the little office where he usually transacted business, holding a newspaper in his hands, and apparently reading. From the expression of his face, as he looked up, it was plain that his thoughts were by no means agreeably occupied. .

"Good morning," said Mr. Strong, cheerfully.

"Good morning," returned Mr. Logan, a kind of growling welcome in his voice. He arose, as he spoke, and offered his visitor a chair.

"A fine day," remarked Mr. Strong.

"Is it?" and Mr. Logan turned his eyes wearily towards the window. "I don't notice the weather half the time, unless, maybe, when it rains, and I can't get out. Any thing new stirring, Mr. Strong?"

"Nothing of special interest."

Mr. Logan sighed heavily, and let his eyes fall to the floor. There were a few moments of silence, when Mr. Strong said:

"You are not well this morning?"

"I can't say that I am ever very well. Between rheumatism and a bad digestion, I never know what it is to feel comfortable in body. But if rheumatism and dyspepsia were all a man had to bear in the world, he might thank God morning and night, and go all day with a cheerful countenance. It is the mind, sir, in which exist the most painful maladies. There are such words as peace, contentment, tranquillity, and the like, but I fear they only express ideal states. Do you know what contentment is, Mr. Strong? Did you ever lie down at night and feel satisfied with the day? I sometimes think that life is a mere cheating

4

dream—that we are the sport of superior be-
ings who laugh at our folly and infatuation."

Mr. Strong had never before seen the rich
man in this frame of mind. He was usually
cold and uncommunicative. Their intercourse
had scarcely ever reached beyond business
themes, and he was, therefore, not a little
surprised at this revelation of himself.

"The words peace, contentment, and tranquillity," said the visitor, "do not, in my
opinion, express mere ideal states; they are
conditions of mind attainable by all, and are
independent of things external."

"I wish that I could think so," replied Mr.
Logan, shaking his head doubtfully.

"It is as true, sir, as that the sun shines.
God made every man for happiness."

"Then his work has proved a signal failure," replied Mr. Logan.

"Man's fault—not God's."

"I will not quarrel with you as to where
the fault lies; the fact is written everywhere
on men's faces. Neither age nor condition is
spared. All—all are wretched."

"But not alike," suggested Mr. Strong. "Some faces we meet lie in perpetual shadow, while others are forever breaking into rippling waves of sunshine."

"There is a difference in temperament, I know," said Mr. Logan, moodily.

"But temperament is not all. It is the quality of a man's life that usually makes his shadows or his sunshine."

"I am not sure that I understand you," and Mr. Logan looked at his visitor curiously.

"And I am not sure that you would understand me if I explained myself." Mr. Strong smiled as he said this.

"Suppose you venture the explanation," and the rich man smiled feebly in return.

After pausing a few moments to collect his thoughts, the visitor said—

"Happiness is not a thing to be sought after as an end. It is simply a resultant state of mind. If our life flows on in heavenly order, happiness comes as a consequence; if adverse to heavenly order, unhappiness is the consequence. I narrow the proposition down to its simplest terms. The question arises, what is heavenly order? and the answer is, that order which is in agreement with the character of man's Creator.· Now, the Bible tells us that God is love. We need not stop to prove that this love is a love of blessing His creatures. It is not self-love, but the love of doing good. God is infinitely wise, good, and happy. Is it not plain that our love must be like His love if we would be wise, good, and happy; a love that seeks to bless others rather than to secure blessings for ourselves?' Mr. Logan, it is because thought is ever turning inward upon the little world of self, and not outward in good-will toward others, that so many of us are discontented. We sow our seed upon a very narrow piece of ground, and the harvest is small, instead of scattering it broadcast over rich fields, that would fill our garners with teeming abundance. God made no single man for himself, but a world full of men, to love and minister to each other and be happy together.   He who withdraws himself into himself, and tries to be happy alone, always fails miserably.   It has been so from the beginning, and will be so to the end.   There is no exception to the rule."

Mr. Logan sat very still, with his eyes upon the floor, while Mr. Strong was speaking.

"There is something in what you say that never came into my thoughts before," said the rich man, lifting his eyes and fixing them steadily on the face of his visitor.

"Turn it over in your mind—look at it upon all sides—ponder it well.   As you live, and as I live, the secret of happiness lies within the compass of what I have said."

The two men sat silent, now, for several minutes, with thoughtful faces.   Believing that to press the subject on the mind of Mr. Logan would be to confuse it, Mr. Strong thought it best to change the theme, and said:

"I was looking at that acre lot of yours down by the factory the other day, and I'll tell you what came into my mind. You know the wretched way in which the mill people live. There is nothing better for them than shanties and miserable hovels, that disgrace the name of houses. Now, you are rich, Mr. Logan, and you would make yourself a public benefactor by laying that acre out into good-sized lots, and covering it with well-built, pleasant little cottages for these poor mill people."

"Are you jesting or in earnest?" Mr. Logan looked at his companion with unfeigned surprise.

"In earnest."

"Humph! I don't see that these mill people have more claims on my benevolence than any of the ten thousand poor wretches that may be picked up within a circle of twenty miles. I may be rich to-day, but if I began the work of squandering my money after that fashion, I would be penniless in less than six months. Oh, no! Mr. Strong, I am not so charitable as that! Let the mill-owners provide proper tenements for their operatives. It is their business, not mine."

"I speak of it as an investment," remarked the other.

"Such as no prudent man would make. I'm too shrewd for an operation of that character," and his eyes gleamed with mingled cunning and intelligence.

"Don't dismiss the subject quite so summarily," said Mr. Strong, smiling. "I think I can show you that the investment I propose will pay handsomely. In a day or two, if you do not object, I will bring plans and specifications that I am sure will interest you. Shall I do so?"

"Oh, certainly, certainly! no harm can be done. Looking at specifications will not commit me to the foolish work of building the cottages."

"So much gained," said Mr. Strong, as he went musing on his way homeward. In a few days he returned to the house of Mr. Logan with his plan for the cottages, in a perspective drawing, that made quite a hand-

some picture. It presented a score of pretty
little houses, each with its neat yard filled
with shrubbery. Mr. Logan was pleased
with the sketch, and listened patiently to all
the conveyancer said on the subject. In the
end he was won over, not, however, we are
free to say, through any benevolent feeling
toward the poor operatives, but because he
saw that pecuniarily the investment would be
a good one.

"So far so good," was the thought of Mr.
Strong. "Once get him fairly into this work,
and his interest in these poor people must be
awakened. My task shall be to keep the
thought of them before him. Humane feelings are almost dead in his heart, but not
past recovery, I hope. There are states of
pity and compassion laid up there in childhood, which, if we can revive them, will stir
its pulses with kind emotions."

Within a month after this improvement of
Mr. Logan's acre lot, near the mill, was sug-
gested, workmen were on the ground. Mr.
Strong had been forward in speaking of the

plan as involving a public benefit, and highly creditable to the projector. Taking the cue, people congratulated Mr. Logan on his liberal spirit, and some made free to tell him that he was the only man in the neighborhood who had let true benevolence go hand in hand with enterprise.

The rich man was flattered by all this, and took credit to himself for a generosity that he did not possess. It was better for him, however, to do good from a selfish end than not to do good at all—better for himself and better for others.

As the cottages progressed, Mr. Logan took more and more interest in them. He was on the ground every day, giving directions to the workmen. Mr. Strong, without seeming to intrude, managed to throw himself in Mr. Logan's way frequently. He always said something pleasant about the little cluster of cottages that were springing up under the hands of busy workmen, as if by magic.

"What a pleasant change it will be for these poor work people," he would remark sometimes ; "how happy they will be ! These light, neat, airy rooms will seem like palace homes to them in contrast with the mean, filthy hovels in which they are now living. Health of mind as well as body will result in the change. And their little children—what a blessed translation for them also ! I seem to hear their voices singing musically from every part of that acre lot, on which pleasant houses are now springing up, where only rank weeds flourished a little while ago. Every good act has its reward, and for this good act yours will surely come."

In due time the cottages were completed. Many little conveniences not at first contemplated were introduced by the proprietor, adding to the cost, but securing greater comfort to the tenants. Some generous feelings were beginning to stir in the heart of the rich man. He was so often praised for his benevolence that he began to wish for the real sentiment, and actually forced himself to make expenditures upon the cottages beyond the original estimates.

On the day Mr. Logan's new tenants took possession of their pleasant homes, he was on the ground, a witness of their delight. It was years since he had felt so all-pervading a sense of pleasure. Mr. Strong was there also, closely observing the rich man, toward whom his feelings of benevolence had moved so earnestly, and, as the sequel had proved, so fruitfully, a year ago.

"Have I done him any good ? Is he any happier than on that day when I looked at his miserable face as he rode in his elegant carriage past Jim Coyle, the tired, discontented day-laborer ? Yes! he is happier, and I trust something better, or, at least, in the way of growing better. But why is he happier ? Because he has made a good investment, and has the interest, or rents, secured to him by the mill-owners ? No. This is not the real source of his better feelings. He is conscious of having done good—of having improved the condition of more than a hundred men, women, and children. It is the thought of this that warms his heart, and sends a pleasant glow through all his being."

Does the reader ask, what of Jim Coyle? Did Mr. Howard try any benevolent experiments with him? Let us see.

Jim Coyle was an Irishman of rather a low order of intellect. He could neither read nor write, and was very little removed from the animal, as to appetites and propensities. He had to work hard at the lowest kind of drudgery, because he was unskilled in any art, and could not be relied upon where thought and intelligence were needed. His tools were the pick-axe and shovel; and a wheelbarrow was the most complicated piece of machinery with which he could be trusted. So Jim Coyle dug cellars and ditches, bent wearily under hods of brick and mortar, trundled heavy loads in his wheelbarrow, broke stones on the roads in the hot July days, and did other useful work of the same laborious character. Jim Coyle was a useful man in his way. If he had possessed more intelligence and more ambition, he might have been useful in a higher degree, when the mind, sharing the body's toil, would have made lighter the burden that rested on his shoulders. But Jim Coyle, like most people, was not fond of work. He knew that he had a hard time of it, and took care that others should know it as well as himself, for he was the most inveterate complainer in the neighborhood. Jim had a wife and two children, and if he had denied himself his tobacco and grog—though we will not say that Jim drank to intoxication—they would have had many more comforts than they now enjoyed.

Mr. Howard, stimulated by the conversation with his neighbor Strong, resolved to befriend this Irishman. So he stopped Jim on the road a day or two afterward, to have a talk with him. The kind interest he manifested drew out Jim, who talked volubly of his hardships and troubles.

"'Dade, 'an yer honor," said Jim, straightening himself up, "this whalin' of stone is the most back-akinist work iver done by mortal mon. Whin I git home at night, I feel as if ivery bone in me body was out ov jint. Och, sure! but it's a misery to live in this way, yer honor. Betther be dead an' lying in the grave—and afther all, not to get more nor enough to kape sowl and body together—to feel the hunger-pain that won't let ye slape at night, yer honor. Ah! sirs, thot's the throuble!"

"How much do you make a day?" asked Mr. Howard.

"Niver more nor a dollar, yer honor, when I have work."

"And you have a wife and two children?"

"Yes, yer honor—Nell and the two babbies, bless their dear sowls!"

"A dollar a day, and not employed all the while?" said Mr. Howard, thoughtfully.

"Thot's all, yer honor, ivery cint—and a wife and two childther to see afther."

"It's a hard case, certainly," remarked Mr. Howard.

"'Dade, and yez may well say thot!" answered Jim.

"Can't you get into some easier work—

something that will give better wages, and be more certain?"

"I don't know, yer honor. There's nobody to care for Jim Coyle, or to spake a word for him when a good siteation is to be had."

"What can you do, Jim?"

"Do, yer honor, is it? Faix, an' a'most ony thing that ony other handy boy can do."

"Very well, Jim," said Mr. Howard encouragingly; "I'll bear you in mind, and if I see any thing lighter and better than your present employment, will put in a good word for you."

"Och! hiven bless yer honor!" ejaculated Coyle, lifting his brimless straw hat. "Yer the first Christian mon that's said a rael Christian word till me these two years. Hiven bless yez!"

Mr. Howard now took up Jim Coyle's case in good earnest, and tried to interest people in his favor; but Jim's character and capabilities were pretty well known throughout the neighborhood, and it was generally thought that he was about as well off as he deserved to be. So Mr. Howard failed to awaken any very decided interest in his protégé. He was getting rather discouraged, when one day a miller, who lived five or six miles distant, asked him if he knew of a good, trusty man, who was out of employment. He wanted him to work about the mill and make himself generally useful, in and out of doors. Among his duties would be the receiving and weighing of grain, and the delivery of flour; and as the mill would have to be left some times entirely in his charge, the miller was particular in saying that the man must be intelligent and trustworthy.

"What wages will you pay?" asked Mr. Howard.

"If a single man," replied the miller, "twenty-two dollars a month and found. If a married man, thirty dollars a month, with a small house and a garden."

Mr. Howard thought a few moments, and then said, against his better convictions—

"I think I know just the man."

"Who, and where is he?" asked the miller.

"He is an Irishman named Coyle, who has been working about here for some time as a common laborer. It is only a few weeks since I was talking with him about his circumstances, and he expressed himself very desirous of getting into a situation where he would be less exposed to the weather and have a more certain income. He lives about a quarter of a mile from here; suppose you call and see him."

"If I were not in such a hurry to get back home," replied the miller, "I would call on him. But I think I may venture to take him on your recommendation."

"Then I will send him over," said Mr. Howard. "I think you'll find him just the man you want. A little awkward, at first, no doubt, but he'll come into your ways and make a valuable assistant."

The miller went on his way, and Mr. Howard sought Jim Coyle, not, it must be owned, without some misgivings as to the Irishman's fitness for the place. Jim was in ecstasies at

5

his promised good fortune, and called upon all the saints in the calendar to shower their blessings on the head of his benefactor. On the next day he went over to the mill with a note from Mr. Howard, and secured the place. The miller was very far from being favorably impressed at first sight, but he knew Mr. Howard very well, had confidence in him, and took his word against his own impressions.

One week after Jim Coyle entered upon his new employment, the miller, who had found him not only stupid, but unreliable, where strict accuracy was important, ventured to leave him in charge of the mill while he went to the landing, two miles distant, to see about some grain he designed purchasing. Very particular directions were given to Coyle about observing the hoppers, lest they should become empty. The head of water was even, the millstones carefully adjusted, and the only thing required was to see that the hoppers were supplied with grain. To make Coyle thoroughly understand what he had to do, the miller, before leaving, took him to the garners above the grinding floor, and explained to him that he must keep the grain well heaped up over the feeding spouts.

For half an hour after the miller left, Coyle stalked about the mill, up stairs and down, with quite a feeling of self-consequence at being in sole charge of the establishment. Walking out, at length, upon the forebay, his eyes were attracted by a multitude of fish swimming about in clear water. He had done some little fishing in the mill-dam since his change of residence, and the sight of two or three large sun-fish threw his mind into quite an excitement. His rod and line, which were in the mill, were brought into immediate requisition, and Jim's vocation changed from that of miller to angler. Millstones, hopper, garner, grain, and all that appertained to miller-craft, vanished from the thoughts of Coyle. He had made a dozen finny captives, and was just casting his hook again, when a terrific explosion in the mill caused him to spring full five feet in the air; a crash and jar followed which seemed as if it would shatter the building to its very foundation.

With an exclamation of terror, Jim started off, running at a wild speed; and but for the timely arrival of neighbors, the building would have been consumed by fire.

The hopper above one of the pairs of millstones had become empty, and the resistance of the grain being lost, the stone revolved with such an increased speed that fire was struck out in the friction of the upper upon the lower stone, and this had set the woodwork surroundings in a blaze. The explosion was occasioned by the bursting of the upper millstone, consequent upon its great velocity. The fragment thrown off weighed over six hundred pounds, and it struck the wall of the building with such violence as to shatter it seriously. The fire was readily extinguished; but the injury occasioned by Jim Coyle's neglect of duty in a position of responsibility, cost the miller over a hundred dollars to repair. It might have cost him thousands.

Thus much for Mr. Howard's benevolent,

but ill-advised attempt to improve the condition of an Irishman who was filling the highest position he could occupy with safety to the interest of others, and who complained of a lot that was the best for him, all things considered.

And so ended the work of this poor man's benefactor, who gave up the case as a hopeless one, and retired ingloriously from the field.

But Mr. Strong's success stimulated him to further efforts in behalf of the "rich repiner," whose unhappy condition had awakened his sympathies.   There could be no peace of mind for him while he lived in angry estrangement from his child, and his benefactor's next effort had in view a reconciliation.

In pursuance of his general purpose, Mr. Strong threw himself frequently into Mr. Logan's way, and showed an intelligent interest in all his affairs that came into view. After a while, Mr. Logan began to talk with him about himself and his affairs more freely than to any other living man. He was naturally suspicious of those who approached him with any degree of familiarity, but Mr. Strong had managed to disarm him, and he was entirely off his guard. He believed the conveyancer to be a true, disinterested friend, and he was right. He was always pleased to converse with Mr. Strong, who had a manly, straightforward, common-sense way of looking at things, and who could demolish a false position, or dissolve a sophism, in such fitting words, that truth became self-evident. To himself, Mr. Logan acknowledged the correction of more than one erroneous view of life, in acting upon which he had aforetimes met sad disappointments.

One day, some three or four months after the completion of the cottages, Mr. Logan and Mr. Strong stood together upon a gently rising piece of ground not far from the academy conducted by his son-in-law, between whom and himself not a word had passed since the day of his daughter's marriage. The piece of ground was owned by Mr. Logan.

"Why don't you build here?" asked Mr.

Strong. "I have always thought this one of the most beautiful sites in the neighborhood."

"It is a beautiful site," replied Mr. Logan; "but why should I build here?" He looked at Mr. Strong as he said this, as if he suspected that there was something in his mind.

"It would be such a handsome improvement," was suggested, "and if the house were not too costly it would readily find a purchaser."

A shadow darkened over the rich man's face. Mr. Strong saw his lips close tightly, and noticed that his hands were shut, and that the fingers worked uneasily against the palms.

"No, sir," he answered, with marked feeling—"no, sir; I will not sell this property, sir!" and he turned suddenly upon Mr. Strong, his countenance showing much agitation. "Sir! I bought this piece of ground more than twenty-six years ago—bought it on the day my daughter was one. year old—bought it for her!" The muscles of his face quivered

almost convulsively. He paused, still looking at his companion steadily—"No, sir"—
more emphatically, "I will not sell this lot so
long as I live !"

This was a revelation not expected by
Mr. Strong. He saw deeper into the heart
of the rich man than he had ever seen before, and gained a knowledge of what he
knew would give him increased power over
him—a power that he meant to use only for
good.

They walked down from that greenly swell-
ing eminence in silence, and neither spoke
again until they had reached a point where
their ways divided. Then, as they stood still
again, Mr. Strong said—

"You are right, sir—do not sell that property ; but"—and he looked earnestly at Mr.
Logan—"for all that, build !"

They had clasped hands, as friends do,
about parting. Nothing more was then
said ; but they looked at each other steadily
for a few moments, hand closed tightly upon
hand—then the grip was relaxed, they turned

from one another, and each went his own way.

"Build—build!" murmured the rich man to himself as he walked slowly homeward; "what does he mean?" Some light must have dawned upon his mind, giving birth to a purpose; for one day, about three weeks afterward, as Mr. Strong was passing in the neighborhood of the ground just mentioned, he was surprised to see half a dozen men busily at work. On approaching nearer, he perceived that they were digging for the foundation of a house.

"So you are going to build," said he to Mr. Logan, on meeting him two or three days afterward.

"Yes; your suggestion pleased me on reflection. The spot is beautifully situated, and I mean to improve it handsomely."

As Mr. Logan did not seem disposed to communicate any thing further at the time, Mr. Strong was careful not to press him with any questions.

Steadily the new improvement went on;

and at the end of four or five months an elegant and commodious house stood forth in all
its fair proportions. Then the grounds were
laid out in the most tasteful style, choice shade
and fruit trees were planted, and vines and
shrubbery scattered around in liberal profu-
sion. It seemed as if Mr. Logan did not know
where to rest the work of ornament.

One day he was standing alone on the piazza of the house, looking over a grassy lawn
that stretched away to a pleasant little sum-
mer-house, against which newly planted vines
were just beginning to spread out their delicate green leaves, when a little boy, about six
years old, came singing along one of the
gravelled walks. The child did not see Mr.
Logan until he came within a few feet of him.
Then he stood still and looked up into his
face. He had dark, lustrous blue eyes, a
broad, white forehead, and a soft, loving
mouth. At first there was a startled look in
the child's countenance, and a shadow like
fear in his eyes ; but these vanished in a
moment ; he came a step or two nearer, still

looking up at Mr. Logan; then paused again and said, in a musical voice, and in a free, confident way,

"Ain't you my grandpa?"

Nothing could have taken Mr. Logan more by surprise than this question. In the hardness of his heart he had refused even to notice his daughter's children, although their grandmother occasionally brought one and another of them home with her, in the faint hope that their presence might stir in his heart some tender emotions. But Mr. Logan had suspected her motive, and so held himself sternly aloof. He did not, therefore, know this child when its tender little face was first uplifted to his. But the word "grandpa" went like an electric throb to the centre of being. There was no mistaking the child—his daughter's eyes looked up into his. A strange softness came over him, a tenderness that seemed foreign to his nature; his heart swelled in his bosom; his vision was dimmed. For some moments he stood looking at the fair creature before him, with no answer upon his tongue. Then sitting down he reached out both hands, and the child came and laid his soft little hands within them, still looking up, half doubtingly, half lovingly, in the old man's face.

"Ain't you my grandpa?" The question was repeated more earnestly than at first.

The fingers of Mr. Logan closed tightly on the little hands that lay within them, and bending down, he left a kiss on the boy's pure forehead.

"I knew you was my grandpa," said the child innocently, and he began stroking Mr. Logan's beard and patting his cheeks in a fond, familiar way. Every touch of that little hand was like a giant's stroke against the ice barrier which pride, selfishness, and avarice had built up between him and his long es- tranged daughter—and in a few moments it lay upon the earth in ruins.

"Who's going to live here, grandpa?" asked the little one. Now that he had made terms with the stern old man, at whom he had only looked, heretofore, timidly, and at a distance, the questioning spirit of childhood began to run free.

"Somebody," replied Mr. Logan, giving a smile of encouragement.

"Who is somebody?" was asked, with that earnestness we see in children.

"You shall know one of these days," and Mr. Logan moved his hand caressingly over the little one's head, and played musingly with the soft curls of his sunny hair.

"Willie! Willie!" a voice in anxious tones suddenly startled the old man. He looked around, but saw no one.

"Here I am, mamma," answered back the child, without stirring from his place. In the next moment a woman, with a half-frightened face, came into view around one of the angles of the house, and stood still within a few feet of Mr. Logan. She clasped her hands and looked at him with a surprised, eager, hopeful expression on her countenance, as fixed, for a moment, as a marble statue. She had come at the right time. Mr. Logan extended his arms and said—

"Oh, Helen!" with a gush of feeling in his voice that swept aside every thing that stood between him and his child. The next instant Helen lay sobbing on his bosom.

It happened that Mr. Strong was passing that way, and that he had turned in from the road a little while before to look at the new building; and it happened that he came in view of the piazza in time to witness that touching scene. It was sacred to them alone, and he retired quickly, without being observed. A week later, and the reconciliation of Mr. Logan with his daughter and her husband was the talk of the neighborhood. Everybody seemed pleased; and it was a common remark that the old man had a softened look, and a kinder manner than had been observed in him for years.

The improvement around the new house went steadily onward; then the work of furnishing began, under the supervision of Mrs. Logan.

"For whom is all this?" asked Mr. Strong, with a pleasant smile, as he looked in one day at the new dwelling, and admired the tasteful elegance with which it was furnished in every part.

Mr. Logan took his hand, and pressed it warmly, saying—

"You have guessed, of course. Do you remember that day you said to me 'build?' My mind was just then groping about in the dark, trying to find the right way. That word gave me the clue, and I have found it. I said that I would never sell this ground, and I will not. I bought it for my child, and it is hers. May God make us both happier than we have been for the last ten years—me especially, for in this long estrangement I have been the most wretched of the two. Mr. Strong! I call you my benefactor; for your suggestions, your leadings, your wise, true, earnest words, fitly spoken, have led me on, step by step, though I knew not whither my feet were tending, until I stand this day where I never thought to stand in this world. I am a happy father, and, compared with what I have been in times past, a happy man. I thank you from my heart! I

repeat, you are my benefactor, and in blessing me you have made me the instrument of
blessing many others.   May your reward be
sweet !"

And it was sweet.

III.

MORE NICE THAN WISE.

A CARRIAGE stopped at the door, the bell was rung, and a few moments afterwards Amy Leslie had her arms around the neck of dear, good Aunt Phœbe.

"Oh! I am so glad to see you! I am so glad you've come!" exclaimed Amy, her face glowing with pleasure.

The old lady kissed her niece; then held her off and looked at her with motherly tenderness.

"Not a bit changed! It is two years since you were married, and your cheeks are as round and blooming, and your eyes as bright as when I last looked into them. A happy wife, I see. And why not? John Leslie was always a good son, and I have no fear about his making a good husband. He was a pet of mine, you know."

6

"Yes, I remember," said Amy, as she drew her arm within Aunt Phœbe's and led her up stairs. "He was your pattern young man. But he isn't perfect. You don't know people till you've lived with them."

Aunt Phœbe stopped and looked into Amy's face a little curiously.

"Oh, you needn't fix your sharp eyes on me after that fashion!" said Amy, laughing. "Men are no more perfect than women."

"Husbands should be perfect in the eyes of their wives," remarked Aunt Phœbe.

"And wives perfect in the eyes of their husbands?"

"Of course."

"Then we are exceptions," said Amy, as they entered the chamber prepared for Aunt Phœbe; "for neither of us thinks the other perfect."

Amy laughed again a gay little laugh—the sound of which was not pleasant to the old lady's ears.

"How is John?" she asked.

"Oh, he's well; and will be so glad to see you."

"How does he get along in business?"

"Very well, I believe. But he complains of being worked half to death."

"He's young and strong," said Aunt Phœbe, "and closeapplication to business won't hurt him."

"But he comes home so tired out as to be right down ill-natured sometimes. And I don't like that."

"I'm sorry," was all Aunt Phœbe replied, and then asked for the baby.

"Oh, he's sweet!" and a gleam of sunshine irradiated the young mother's countenance. "Come; he's sleeping in the next room;" and she drew Aunt Phœbe into the chamber, where her baby-treasure lay. "Isn't he lovely, Aunt?"

"Dear angel!" said the old lady, bending over the crib, and gazing with delighted eyes upon the rosy infant.

"And so John is a little cross sometimes?"

remarked Aunt Phœbe, as they sat together in the sitting-room, not long afterwards.

"Yes; cross as a bear now and then, if I must say so," replied Amy.

"Oh, not so bad as that," said Aunt Phœbe. "Cross as a bear is pretty strong language. I can't believe it of John."

Amy's face grew serious; then fell into deeper shadow.

"What's the matter, dear? You don't look happy. Nothing wrong, I hope?" and Aunt Phœbe laid her hand on Amy's arm and looked at her rather anxiously.

"Oh, no—nothing very wrong. But——" and Amy paused.

"But what? nothing *very* wrong? Then there is *something* wrong?"

"Well, the truth is, Aunt Phœbe, John isn't as amiable and good-tempered as he used to be. He's careless and disorderly about the house; and if I say a word to him he gets into a huff. Now, if there's one thing I do like, it is order and neatness at home; and

John tries me dreadfully. I don't know what has come over him."

"I'm sorry!"

It was Aunt Phœbe's only remark on that subject at the time. But she determined to look on with open eyes and see where the evil lay, that was casting already a shadow upon the heart of her niece.

"John will be home in a little while," said Amy, as the twilight began to fall. "Ah, there is his key in the door, and that's his step in the passage;" and she went out to meet him, closing the room door after her.

Aunt Phœbe listened as they moved along the passage to where the hat-rack stood.

"There!" she heard her niece say, in rather an unamiable tone; "don't throw your hat down on the chair. Why don't you hang it up?"

John made some reply, but she did not hear it distinctly. His voice struck her as being a little rough.

"On that lower peg again! Don't you see that your coat touches the floor?"

"It won't hurt the floor," came to Aunt Phœbe's ears, in an annoyed tone.

"Incorrigible!" responded Amy.

A few moments of silence followed. Then she heard her niece say :

"Aunt Phœbe is in the parlor."

In the next instant the door flew open. John hurried across the room, and, grasping Aunt Phœbe's hand, said with warmth :

"This is a pleasure! How glad I am to see you!" and he held her hand tightly, and looked fondly into her face.

A crowd of questions and answers followed each other closely on both sides, in the midst of which Amy broke in with :

"Don't put your foot on the round of that chair, John ; you'll rub the varnish off."

John removed his foot without making any answer. But Aunt Phœbe saw his brow gather slightly, with a sign of displeasure. They went on talking, and presently the young man, who had taken a seat near the window, took hold of the cord which looped back the curtain, and commenced running it through his fingers.

"You'll fray that cord, John," said Amy. "Do let it alone !"

John still kept it in his hand as if he had not heard her, and still toyed with it in an absent way.

"John ! don't ! You'll ruin that cord."

Mr. Leslie dropped it, without looking towards his wife or replying, and still kept on talking with Aunt Phœbe.

Soon, in his earnestness, the young man forgot himself again. Grasping a chair which stood near him, and balancing it upon one leg, he moved it backwards and forwards with a see-sawing motion. Amy's sense of propriety was outraged again. The act annoyed her, and she could not repress her annoyance. This time she said nothing. but reached towards the chair, and attempted to remove it from his hand. John did not choose to let it go, however. Amy drew firmly on the chair, and he held on to it firmly.

"Let me have the chair!" said the persistent little woman.

"Do you wish to sit down in it?" said
John, looking up steadily into her face.

"No, but——"

"But what?" asked her husband, knitting
his brows.

"Why will you play with chairs in that
fashion?" said Amy, with slight irritation.
"It makes me nervous to see you."

"I'm sorry your nerves are so delicate,"
said John Leslie, pushing away the chair.
"My wife, Aunt, has grown as particular as
an old maid."

Aunt Phœbe made no reply. She felt uncomfortable. For nearly a minute silence
pervaded the room. Then the tea-bell rung,
and the scene changed. They were scarcely
seated at the table before John was guilty of
some little breach of etiquette which brought
on him a reproving word from his wife. He
did not seem to notice her.

"Why, husband, how can you do so?"
broke from her lips a few moments after-

wards. " You really seem to be trying yourself."

"What has he done, child?" said Aunt
Phœbe, looking across the table in some surprise at Amy.

"Done? Just look at his cup on the table-
cloth. A nice stain it will make."

"Where are you cup-plates?" asked Aunt
Phœbe.

"Oh, dear! nobody has cup-plates now-a-
days," answered Amy.

"That's just it, Aunt," said John. "Our
Amy is growing excessively genteel. She
won't have cup-plates, and I'm not the fool to
burn my mouth with hot tea and coffee. Both
being self-willed, there has as yet been no
compromise."

"Nonsense, children!" spoke out Aunt
Phœbe. "This is a little worse than trifling."
The old lady's rebuking tone rather chilled
them, and neither made any additional remark.
But the buoyancy of their feelings was gone,
and was not fully restored during meal-
time. After supper they all went up stairs

into a cosy sitting-room. They were there only a few minutes, when John commenced drawing off one of his boots, saying as he did so :

"How my poor feet do ache. They've been bound up in this tight leather since morning."

"Don't take them off here!" exclaimed Amy. "Do go over into our room! Your slippers are there."

But he paid no more attention to his wife than if he had not heard her. The boot just removed he placed against the wall, and went on deliberately taking off the other.

"There, that feels better," he said. "I tell you what, Aunt Phœbe, it's no joke to go all day with a pair of tight boots on. My feet feel as if taken out of a vice."

"Well, I'm downright ashamed of you, John Leslie !" said his wife.

"I hope you will never have any thing worse to be ashamed of," he replied, and not in a very kind tone of voice. "I think it's a pity if I can't take my boots off where I please in my own house."

"Oh, as to that," retorted Amy, her face reddening, "you can take them off in the parlor if you choose, and put them on the What-not for an ornament! I don't care."

"I'm glad to hear you say that," retorted John.

"You are?" said Amy, sharply.

"Yes; I shall have some peace of my life now."

"I don't understand you," said Amy, showing some irritation of manner.

"Oh, it's very plain," answered the young man. "If I can leave my boots in the parlor, I can leave them anywhere. Much obliged to you for condescending so much."

And he laughed in a mocking way that was particularly irritating to his wife, who lost temper, and said a good many hard, accusing things to her husband; and then, giving way to a passionate flood of tears, left the room.

"Is that right, John?" said Aunt Phœbe, looking soberly into the young man's face.

"Is what right?"

"Right for you to do what is annoying to your wife?"

"She's no right to be annoyed with trifles of this kind," he answered firmly.

"That is not speaking like a kind and sensible man, John. Your wife is neat and orderly by nature, and cannot help being annoyed at what is disorderly. This is not the place for your boots."

"I know it, Aunt. But when a man's tired half to death on coming home, he might be excused for pulling his boots off anywhere."

"Yes, if he were more thoughtful of himself than anybody else. But we won't discuss this matter now. I must go to Amy, poor child!"

And Aunt Phœbe arose and went from the sitting-room, leaving John Leslie in no very comfortable frame of mind. She found Amy in her own apartment, sitting on the side of her bed, sobbing violently. Aunt Phœbe sat down by her, and taking one of her hands, said:

"As soon as you have grown calm enough to listen to me, I wish to say a few words."

Amy sobbed more violently for a little while; and then, the paroxysm abating, she became still and silent.

"Are you ready to hear me?" asked Aunt Phœbe.

"Yes," came faintly from Amy's lips.

"In the first place then," began the old lady, "I would like to know if it is in this way that you receive your tired husband, every evening, when he returns from business?"

"In what way, Aunt Phœbe? I don't understand you."

"In a fault-finding way, I mean."

"But, Aunt, I cannot let him act in such a disorderly manner."

"Stop, my child!" said Aunt Phœbe. "You are wrong. The love of your husband is more to you than these trifles. If his heart is all right; if he is manly, honorable, and kind; do not these qualities far outweigh the small defects of which you complain? You did not meet him to-night when he came home with tender words, but in reproof. It would have been but a little thing for you to have hung up his hat when he placed it thoughtlessly on the chair ; or to have raised his coat to a higher position on the rack, if he left it too low for your fancy. You would both have felt happier for this forbearance and attention on your part, and surely your own peace of mind and the happiness of your husband are things to be first considered. What is the varnish on a chair-round to the smile of your husband ?. Or the freshness of a tassel-cord to his tender and loving thought of you? Why, child, you are throwing away precious gems for glitter and tinsel. Wasting love and gathering up bitterness of heart for the time to come. How much better would it have been, when he drew off his boots in the sitting-room, and complained of their tightness and of his weariness, for you to have said to him, in kind consideration : 'I will take your boots, John, and get your slippers.' That would have been wifely and lovingly done; and he would have rewarded you with a gratified smile. But how does it stand now? He is angry and you are unhappy. Are a few little home-proprieties to be valued more than love and peace?"

Aunt Phœbe paused. Amy looked at her for some moments in a half-startled, half-bewildered way, as if a new and accusing truth were breaking in upon her mind. Then she laid her face down against her and wept for some time silently.

"Am I not right, my child?" said Aunt Phœbe.

Amy lifted her head and answered:

"Yes, you are right, and I have been wrong. Thoughtless, foolish woman! how weak and unwise I have been. Thanks, dear Aunt Phœbe! for your plainly uttered reproof."

When Amy returned to the sitting-room, she had her husband's dressing-gown on her arm, and his slippers in her hand.

"Give me your coat, John," she said, with a pleasant smile, "here is your dressing-gown."

"Oh, you need not have taken that trouble," returned her husband, in surprise.

"It's no trouble, dear," answered his wife, putting her hand on the collar of his coat, and helping him to remove it.

"There," she added, as she drew off the last sleeve, " is your dressing-gown, and here are your slippers. I will take your coat and boots over to the chamber."

All this was so unexpected to John, that the whole thing was done before he had time to object or remonstrate.

There was no more fault-finding on that evening; no more sharp or complaining words; but considerate kindness and gentle attentions from one to the other. It was a long time since the hours had passed so pleasantly. A shadow had fallen over the brightness of their home; a spirit of accusation had come in; alienation had begun; their love-freighted bark had passed from calm waters to a troubled sea; they were in danger of shipwreck; but Aunt Phœbe came at the right moment, and, by fitly spoken words, restored order, harmony, and peace.

IV.

THE ENVIED LOT.

"NOTHING to do but sit at the window and read, to make calls, to receive visitors, or to enjoy herself in any way that suits her fancy. Some people in this world have all the work allotted to them, while others sport like butterflies in the sunbeams. I belong to the working class."

And Mrs. Fulton sighed wearily. She stood, holding a great baby in her arms, looking across the street through the half-drawn curtains, at a neighbor who sat by her parlor window reading. Every day Mrs. Fulton saw her sitting there, neatly dressed and ready for company; almost every day she saw her going out or coming in. She had apparently no work to do, and seemed free from care. Mrs. Fulton envied her. Even as she stood now, looking at her neighbor, a hand pulled

7

vigorously at her dress, and a voice cried, fretfully,

"Mamma! mamma! Jane's got my doll's bonnet, and won't give it to me."

Mrs. Fulton let fall the curtain which she had drawn aside, and turning with a quick movement, said, with some excitement of manner, for she was just in the state of mind to feel disturbing influences,

"Quarrelling again! It is too bad! Why did Jane take your doll's bonnet? What did you do to her?"

"I only pushed over a chair in her baby-house. Shan't she give me my doll's bonnet?"

"Did you push over the chair on purpose?" asked Mrs. Fulton.

"I asked her to let me take it out, and she wouldn't," said the child.

"And then you pushed it over?" Mrs. Fulton looked at her sternly.

"Shan't Jane give me my doll's bonnet? I want my doll's bonnet," and the little girl began to cry passionately.

"Stop this instant!"exclaimed the mother, grasping her arm.

There was menace in her voice, and the child knew by experience that if she did not stop her cries, a blow would, most likely, fall upon her.

Still holding tightly the child's arm, Mrs. Fulton passed with her to the room above, where, a little while before, she had left her children at play.

"Jane," she said, "what is the trouble between you and Mary? Why don't you give her the doll's bonnet."

"Because she knocked over a chair in my baby-house, and wouldn't set it up again." And Jane looked angry and revengeful.

"And so," said the mother, by a sudden effort regaining her self-possession, and speaking in a subdued tone of voice, "you return evil for evil."

"She'd no business to knock over my chair," replied Jane, with scarcely a sign of relenting.

"That is true, my daughter; but as I have

often told you, two wrongs never make a right. I am sorry that, because she acted badly, you have done the same. Mary," and she turned to the younger child, "go and put that chair in its right place."

Mary knew that to hesitate would be to involve her in punishment; so with pouting lips, and a slow, reluctant hand, she obeyed her mother, and put the chair in its right position.

"Now, Jane," added the mother, "give Mary her doll's bonnet."

And that was done, but in no very gracious manner.

Mrs. Fulton tried, now, by a few rightly spoken words, to make her children see the evil of their conduct. But passion blinded both of them, and she made, apparently, no impression.

"Naughty children!" she exclaimed at last, impatiently, losing her own self-control, and turning from them with a sad, bitter feeling in her heart, saying to herself, "I am discouraged! There seems to be no good in them.

Oh, if my children were only kind to one another! If I could see them growing up in love and good will, all of my life's burdens would be easy to bear."

And she sat down with her heart in shadow. Mrs. Fulton had not felt very well since morning. She had risen with a headache, which had accompanied her thus far through the day. It was a dull, deep-seated pain, attended by a disturbance of the whole nervous system, and bringing depression of mind as well as body. As often happens in the best ordered households, every thing had seemed to go wrong for the day. The cook was late with her breakfast, and sent nearly every article of food spoiled to the table. Mr. Fulton complained of his coffee; said something unpleasant about the badly-cooked steak; grumbled over his hard-boiled eggs; and finally left the table and the house in evident ill-humor. Mrs. Fulton did not eat a mouthful —she would have choked in the attempt to swallow food. After leaving the breakfast-table, Mrs Fulton went up stairs to the sitting-room, where she commenced the work of washing and dressing her baby. In the midst of this, and while the baby lay half washed on her lap, John, her oldest boy, who was just ready to start for school, caught his sleeve on a nail, and tore in it a great rent. If she waited to finish washing and dressing the baby before mending this rent, John would be too late for school. So she had to cover the naked baby in her lap while she mended the garment. The child was already out of patience with the washing and dressing business, and now commenced screaming to the full capacity of its lungs. Fretted, in consequence of the torn jacket, and the necessity for mending it under such unfavorable circumstances, and now more fretted with the child's screaming, Mrs. Fulton's head began to ache with greater intensity, the pain almost blinding her.

"Now off to school as fast as you can go!" said the mother, as she pushed John from her, after he had put on the mended jacket. But, instead of leaving the room at once, John commenced rummaging through the book-case.

"Why don't you go to school?" demanded Mrs. Fulton, in a sharp voice.

"I can't find my Philosophy," replied John.

"What did you do with it?"

"I didn't do any thing with it. Somebody's hid it away," answered the boy, in a dogged manner.

"I wish you'd take care of your books," said Mrs. Fulton, fretfully. "There's always some trouble about them. Go and look in your room."

"It isn't there, I know," said the boy positively.

"Then look down in the dining-room.

"I have looked there."

"Well, go and look again."

John went down stairs, but returned, in a little while, saying he could not find the book.

"O, dear! there's always some trouble. Go and look for the book right. It hasn't flown away, nor walked away." Mrs. Fulton spoke with angry impatience.

John went again to the book-case, and

searched deliberately through all the shelves. Then he went to the closet, and reduced things to disorder there, but without finding his Philosophy.

"You'll be late to school," said the worried mother.

"Well, I can't go without my Philosophy."

"What's the reason you can't?"

"I'll be kept in, so I will."

As Mrs. Fulton could not leave off washing the baby to look for John's book, and as John wouldn't go without it, the school hour came and found him still at home. As soon as Mrs. Fulton could lay her baby in the cradle, she went to the book-case, and almost the first object on which her eyes rested, was John's Philosophy.

"Here it is, you troublesome boy! and I've a mind to box your ears. Now run off to school as fast as your feet will carry you."

"I want an excuse," said John, standing firm.

"Tell your teacher the reason why you are late."

"She won't take that excuse. It must be written."

So Mrs. Fulton had to sit down and write an excuse, though her hand trembled so that she could scarcely hold the pen, and her headache was so blinding that she could scarcely see the paper.

After John had gone to school, and Jane and Mary had been enjoined to keep very quiet, and not wake the baby, who was sleeping in the cradle after his morning ablutions, Mrs. Fulton went down into the kitchen to give some directions about dinner, and to say a word to the cook about her morning delinquencies. The cook was far from being in an amiable mood, and on the first word of complaint went off into a passion, and indulged in some very unwarrantable impertinence, at which the lady became naturally indignant. Certain things that she said in a cutting and authoritative way offended madam cook, who gave notice that she would leave on the next day.

As this scene with the cook closed, the curtain rose on another scene of excitement. Jane and Mary had quarrelled, and in their noisy strife awakened the sleeping baby before his nap was half finished. His screams, mingled with the passionate vociferations of Jane and Mary, smote on the ear of poor Mrs. Fulton, as she emerged from the kitchen.

"O dear!" she ejaculated, clasping her throbbing temples. "I shall go crazy with all this," and running up stairs, she silenced the angry children with a sharp reproof and taking up the baby, soothed it to quiet on her breast.

It was a little while after this scene, that she stood at the parlor window, looking through the half-drawn curtain at the envied lady on the other side. Even while she sighed over the heavier burdens that were laid on her weak shoulders, she was called away from the parlor, as the reader has seen, by a renewal of strife among her children. As she sat, after the subsidence of this little storm, in despondency and discouragement, she heard the bell ring. A lady friend had called, and she went down into the parlor to meet her.

"Are you not well?" said the lady, as she took her hand and looked into her pale face, the smile on which did not obliterate all marks of pain.

"Not very well," she replied, the smile fading quite away, and leaving on her countenance an expression of weariness and care. "It is one of my headache days. I have had them ever since I can remember. Time was when I could find a quiet room, and remain undisturbed, until the quivering nerves found rest and ease; but that day passed long ago. There is no rest, nor ease, nor quiet, for a mother. Well or ill, she must be at her post. Ah, my friend; there are times when I feel that my lot is a hard one; that my burdens are heavier than I can bear."

And Mrs. Fulton, overcome for the moment, by her feelings, gave way to tears.

The friend sat silent until she had a little recovered herself, and then offered some words of comfort; but they did not reach the

heart of Mrs. Fulton.   She was in a complaining and desponding mood.   The current of
her thoughts had taken a wrong direction,
and no light word could turn it back again.
The comforting suggestions of her friend were
pushed aside as of no value.

"It is work, work, toil, toil, early and late,
sick or well, fresh or weary.   That is my lot,
and I think it a hard one.   Look at Mrs.
H——, sitting idly by the window opposite,
dressed for company, and with nothing to do
but to read, visit, and go out and come in at
her own good pleasure."

"And yet," answered the friend, "your
lot is blessed and your home a paradise compared with hers.   Did you ever study her
face ?   There, look at it now.   She has lifted her
eyes from the book—I doubt if her thought is
on its pages.   Notice her mouth.   She cannot
see us as we stand behind this curtain, and
gaze through the small opening.   Did you
ever see a sadder expression ?"

"It is sad," said Mrs. Fulton, "very sad.
I never noticed it before."

"Patient and sad," remarked the friend, in a tone of sympathy.

"Do you know her?" asked Mrs. Fulton.

"Not personally. But I know something of her life and history, and there are some passages, that I can never think of without shuddering. She is not happy with her husband, and never can be. Ten years ago she was engaged to a young man, between whom and herself existed the tenderest passion. Mr. H——, who is now her husband, addressed her at the same time with the young man to whom I have referred, but she declined his suit and favored that of the other. Her father was on the side of Mr. H——, who was wealthy; but she was true to her lover against all opposition from her parents, and all overtures on the part of Mr. H——.

"Unwilling to marry without the full approval of her parents, the union of the lovers was deferred from month to month, until nearly two years of patient waiting had elapsed, when a free consent being still withheld, the marriage was about being consummated in the face of all opposition.

"Just one week before her appointed wedding-day, the young man was arrested for the crime of forgery. Under these circumstances, the ceremony was, of course, put off. Notwithstanding the young man's persistent declaration of innocence, there was sufficient evidence on the trial to convict him, and he was sentenced to the State's Prison for five years. It was nearly a year before the almost broken-hearted girl again appeared in society. Mr. H—— then renewed his attentions, and pressed his suit so earnestly, that, in time, she yielded, what most persons believed, a reluctant consent. They were married. A year afterwards, some friends of the unhappy young man, who still lay in prison, received intimations from an unknown source, that there had been foul play: that he was really innocent of the crime for which he had been sentenced to a fearful expiation. Enough was communicated to put them on the right track of investigation. Having the clue, they followed it steadily, but surely, until the whole mystery was unravelled. Sufficient evidence was obtained, to show that the forgery was committed by some other person; and this person, while concealing himself under an assumed name, gave such a clear detail of facts and circumstances bearing on the case, as left no doubt whatever of the young man's innocence, and he was immediately pardoned by the governor. But the information received did not stop here; it charged H—— with being an accomplice in the matter; not as a sharer in the crime, so far as receiving a portion of the money was concerned, but as an adviser of the ways and means, by which an innocent young man was convicted and sent to prison. There was not sufficient evidence against him for legal prosecution, but in the minds of all who looked closely into the matter, he was considered guilty of one of the basest crimes that can stain human nature.

"It is said that the young man, on being released from prison, went to the house of Mr.

H——, and charged him, in the presence of his wife, with the dastardly crime of which he had been guilty; alleging, at the same time, that he had all the proofs of his complicity, and would not only expose him before the world, but prosecute him to the law's fullest extent. It is said further, that his appeal to Mrs. H——, on this occasion, was of the most agonizing character, and that she was so shocked as to lose all consciousness and lie insensible for many hours. Friends interposed to prevent any public exposure of the matter. The young man, whose innocence was made clear, returned to his old social position, and assumed his old business relations. A few years ago, he married one of the loveliest girls in our city. He lives only in the next block, and few days pass, I think, in which Mrs. H—— does not see his sweet young wife and pleasant child go past her window."

The lady paused, looking still into the face or Mrs. Fulton.

"You envied Mrs. H——, a little while

ago," she continued, "are you ready to exchange places with her now?"

"No—no—no!" said Mrs. Fulton with much feeling. "You said truly, that my lot was blessed and my home a paradise compared with hers. Exchange places? God forbid! I would sink down and die under the burden that rests upon her heart."

"We have all our burdens," said the friend. "You have your burdens and I have mine; and sometimes they seem heavy and hard to bear. But oh, they are light as thistle-down compared with what some others have to endure. You have a kind, honorable husband, and children, of whom any mother might be proud—not sinless cherubs, of course, but touched with faults and evil inclinations, that require their mother's care, discipline, and patience. If she is faithful to her high responsibilities, great will be her reward —rich her blessing."

"Thank you, my kind, wise friend," said Mrs. Fulton, light breaking over her face, "I stand corrected; you have taken a mist from

before my eyes, and I see things in new and
truer relations. Poor Mrs. H——! Is the
case indeed so sad with her? There is no
compensation in ease and leisure for a trouble like hers. If I am worn and weary with
my day's work, I can lie down at night
in peace, and sleep. If I am sometimes
fretted at the faults of my children, how
much oftener is my heart full of gladness,
in their tender love? Have I not cause for
thankfulness? And yet I have been mur-
muring over a lot that is full of blessing.
Thanks for the lesson you have taught me.
I shall be wiser in the time to come."

THE TWO LEGACIES.

THE chamber in which the sick man lay was small, and the furniture poor, though every thing was, neat, clean, and orderly. There were four persons in the room; the sick man, his wife, and two children. The elder of the children was a boy fifteen years of age; the other, a girl just entering her sixth year. They were standing around the bed, gazing with tearful eyes upon a beloved face, which, after a few more feeble heart-beats, would be cold and expressionless.

"Edward," said the dying man, taking the hand of his son, and looking at him with a tender, yearning solicitude; "Edward, my son, I am now about to leave you. It has not pleased our good Father in heaven to make me rich; I have neither houses, nor lands, nor money for my children—only the legacy of a good name, which I hand over to you as a sacred trust. Look well to it, that nothing sullies its brightness. Keep it as our family heir-loom, and transmit it undimmed to your children. If you are ever tempted to do wrong, think of this high trust, and forbear. Be honest, virtuous, industrious, temperate, and faithful to all trusts that may be confided to you; and if it is best for you to gain riches in this world, God will pour them into your lap; and if you remain virtuous and honorable, holding them as good gifts from above, they will bless instead of cursing you. You are only a boy, but your hands are already used to work, and have acquired some skill. Be faithful to your employer, as if the business were your own. I leave your mother and sister in your care. Never forget them, my son."

Then laying his thin white hand on the boy's head, the dying man, with his dim eyes lifted upwards, said, tremulously—

"The Lord bless thee, my son; and keep thee, unspotted, in this evil world."

An hour afterwards, and there was silence and desolation in the house.

In the same street, and directly opposite, towered the stately mansion of one who had been more favored by worldly fortune. And his time had come also.. Death is no respecter of persons. In his eyes, all are equal; rich and poor; the lofty and the humble; the bond and free—all alike must go down with naked feet to the darkly flowing river. Around his bed were gathered wife, and children, and friends. But the dying man's legacy was not reserved for announcement at this late moment. Years before, in due legal form, his last will and testament had been written. His son and daughter would inherit ample fortunes. And so, in these his last moments, no anxious thoughts for them held him lingering on the utmost verge of mortality. Gradually his pulses grew feebler and feebler, and he died without a word or sign.

Almost at the same moment, a small piece of crape was fastened on a dingy brass doorknob, and a sign of death, falling in ample folds to the very door-step, tied to a silver bell-handle. From opposite sides of the street, these tokens of death looked at each other; the one fluttering bravely in the wind, the other shrinking against the door, as if half ashamed of its office. Three days afterwards, a grand funeral ·cortege, stretching away in a line of thirty carriages, took up its solemn march towards a fashionable cemetery. An hour later, and a hearse and two carriages moved sadly from the little house opposite the one from which the great company of mourners had passed.

Edward Strong and Charles Raynor, orphaned by these two deaths, were of nearly the same age. But how different their lots, and how different their prospects! To each had passed a legacy; but of what a different character!

———

In a work-shop, leaning over a bench, sat a boy. His clothes were coarse; his hands soiled and rough; his face dark with smoke and sweat. But all his movements were quick, and showed his mind to be active and in earnest. There were others at work around him—boys and men; some active and in earnest, like himself; others with slower and less interested movements, and some idling, or but half employed. The door opened, and the owner of the shop entered. He had a quick eye, and at a glance understood, from the movement of every boy and man, with what degree of earnestness he had been employed. To one he spoke a sharp word; to another he gave a mild reproof; and then came and stood by the lad to whom we have just referred. The boy did not look up, nor quicken his motions, but kept on in his earnest way. While the man yet stood looking at him, he finished the piece of work on which he was engaged. His employer took it from his hands, and after examining it carefully, for a little while, said in a kind, approving voice,

"Very well done, indeed, Edward, and finished in good time. Take it into the store; there's a job that I want done by a careful hand.   I will be down in a few moments to see you about it."

The boy arose from his bench, with a glow of pleasure ruddily gleaming through the soil on his cheeks, and passed from the shop with an elastic step.   The proprietor came down into the store a few minutes afterwards, but, before noticing the boy, he went to a clerk who stood writing at a desk, and said to him,

" How much do we pay Edward Strong ?"

The clerk took down a book, and, on referring to it, answered,

"Three dollars a week, sir."

" Make it five."

"Yes, sir ;" and the book was closed.

The man, whom we will call Mr. Campbell, turned from the desk, and went to where Edward was standing, awaiting his pleasure.

"We took an order this morning, Edward," said Mr. Campbell, "from a very particular customer, and I want it done in the neatest manner."

He then gave Edward a description of the article required, with a pattern to work from.

There were certain deviations from the pattern, however, that only an intelligent mind could comprehend, and a skilled hand execute. After a full description had been given, Mr. Campbell said,

"Can you do it, Edward?"

The boy lifted his bright, intelligent eyes to his employer's face, and answered, in a confident tone, "I can try, sir."

"It is wanted on the day after to-morrow. The time is short; do you think it can be done?"

"Yes, sir, by working at night."

Mr. Campbell stood a moment, and then said,

"You think it will require night-work?"

"I wouldn't like to risk not getting it done," replied Edward; "so I'll come back to-night, after supper, and get ahead as far as possible. With this start, I can finish it to morrow, or at least to-morrow night. You may depend on it, sir, if I am alive and well."

When Edward went home at the close of that week, he took the good news to his mother that his wages had been raised to five dollars, and that Mr. Campbell said he was the best and trustiest workman among all his apprentices. It was an hour of joy to that mother, who sat low down in the vale of poverty, with the shadow of a great affliction resting upon her.

———

At his desk sat a boy dressed in fine broadcloth, leaning over a book, but only pretending to study. A recitation was called, and he went up with his class. When his turn came to recite, he was dumb. The teacher prompted him, when he blundered over a few sentences and then came to a full stop. The fact was, he had only pretended to study his lesson, and, as a consequence, did not know it. The teacher reproved him before the class, and the boy answered impertinently.

"Charles Raynor," said the teacher, in a stern voice, "you must take back that word instantly!

The boy stood silent and dogged.

"Did you understand me, sir? There must be an instant apology before the class."

The boy looked defiant. There was no thought of apology in his mind. He, Charles Raynor, with a legacy of sixty thousand dollars, to come into his hands on the day he became twenty-one years of age—he knew the exact provisions of his father's will—he apologize to a poor schoolmaster? No, indeed!

The teacher stood, sternly awaiting his decision.

"I give you five seconds, sir!"

The boy looked up with an insolent leer.

"Take your hat and go home, sir," said the teacher, as the five seconds expired.

The boy turned and left the school-room.

Mrs. Raynor was far from approving the conduct of her son, and tried her best to make him return and offer a suitable apology to the teacher. But the lad had already grown purse-proud, and was not going to humiliate himself to a "beggarly schoolmaster," as he was pleased to call an accomplished and high-minded teacher, who occupied a more elevated position than it was possible for him ever to gain.

Five years later. In the same room where Edward Strong had received the legacy of a good name, with the dying injunction and blessing of his father, sat, late in the evening, a young man, deeply absorbed in a book. It was Edward himself, now on the verge of manhood. He had grown tall and well-developed in chest and limb. His face was thoughtful, intelligent and grave, for one of his years; his eyes large, deep, earnest, and full of purpose, as you would have acknowledged, had you seen them, as he looked up from his book on the entrance of his mother. He smiled as he closed the volume and said,

"Sit down, mother."

As Mrs. Strong sat down, Edward continued: "When father died he left me his good name. Its lustre is not tarnished yet, and God being my helper, it never shall be! I cannot forget that hour, nor what my father said to me a little while before his voice grew forever silent on the earth. It was a legacy better than gold. He said, 'Be honest, virtuous, industrious, and temperate,' and ever since that time I have seemed to hear his voice repeating the injunction. I have not been without temptation, but a thought of him always gave me strength to overcome, and so, dear mother, I have conquered thus far, though many have fallen around me. There was another injunction which I have endeavored strictly to obey. He said, ' Be faithful to your employer as if the business were your own.' I have endeavored to be thus faithful, and this faithfulness has worked to my own benefit in many ways, and now, especially, in this: To-day Mr. Campbell made me foreman of the shop, and increased my wages to eighteen dollars a week, saying to me at the same time, such kind and flattering things as covered my cheeks with blushes."

"There is no happier mother than I am to-night," said Mrs. Strong, as she clasped the hands of her son, and held them tightly against her breast.

Even at this moment there came a loud, riotous cry from the street in front of their dwelling, startling mother and son from their present state of mind. On going to the window and looking out, they saw a young man struggling in the hands of a police officer.

"Charles Raynor, as I live!" exclaimed Edward.

"What is the matter with him?" asked Mrs. Strong, in an alarmed voice.

"Drunk, that is all," said Edward, as he saw the young man throw his arms above his head, and heard him cry out in a voice that was incoherent from intoxication.

At this moment the door of Mrs. Raynor's elegant mansion opened, and a waiter came out hurriedly. Seizing an arm of the young man, he drew him, with the assistance of the policeman, into the house. The door shut, and the policeman retired.

"Wretched mother!" said Mrs. Strong, in a tone of pity, as she turned from the window with tears in her eyes. "How my heart aches for her!"

———

A few months later Mr. Campbell stood talking with Edward in the shop, on some

matter of business. He had finished what he
had to say, and was about turning from the
young man, when, from the impulse of some
thought, presenting itself at the moment, he
asked,

"How old are you, Edward?"

"I am twenty-one to-day," was replied.

"Ah! then you are of age?"

"Yes, sir."

"I congratulate you on attaining your ma-
jority," said Mr. Campbell, taking Edward's
hand, and grasping it warmly. "If the promise of your boyhood is fulfilled, success and
honor lie before you. Since the day you
came into my shop as a boy, I have never had
aught against you."

"I have tried always to do my duty," said
the young man modestly.

"And you have not failed. But what are
your plans as to the future?" said Mr. Campbell.

"I have no plans, sir."

"I should like you still to hold your present situation."

"I have no wish to change," was replied.

"You have made my interests your own," said Mr. Campbell, speaking slowly, like a man who desired his words to be understood and remembered, "and hereafter your interests shall be mine. Remember that I am in earnest, Edward," and turning away he left the shop.

What a happy mother was Mrs. Strong on that birthday evening of her son, when he repeated to her the words of Mr. Campbell! Her heart beat in great throbs of pleasure, and swelled with pride and gratitude.

"O, my son!" she exclaimed, "you have made my cup brimming with joy."

———

It was three or four weeks subsequent to this time, when a young man, fashionably dressed, entered the office of a prominent citizen, and said to an attendant, in a curt, half insolent way.

"Is Mr. H—— in?"

"He is," replied the attendant.

"Then I wish to see him."

"Will you take a seat, sir? He is engaged just now."

"How long will he be engaged?" asked the young man, rudely.

"Not long. Sit down."

The visitor muttered something impatiently, and commenced walking the floor in a restless way. After a few minutes he turned to the attendant and said,

"Go and tell Mr. H—— that Charles Raynor wishes to see him."

The attendant went into the next room, and returned in a few moments, saying that Mr. H—— would be at leisure in five minutes. At the end of this time a gentleman, with whom Mr. H—— had been engaged, came out, when the young man passed in.

"Good morning, Charles," said Mr. H——, smiling, and extending his hand, as his visitor entered. Mr. H—— was a man somewhat past middle age, with a face that indicated solidity of character, united with an intelligent experience of life. The smile with which he greeted the young man, played for only a mo-

9

ment or two about his lips, when his look became grave.

"I suppose," said Charles, as he sat down at the request of Mr. H——, "you are aware that I am of age to-day."

"Yes, Charles, I am aware of it," replied Mr. H——.

"And you are also aware," said Charles, "that according to my father's will I am now to receive my share of his estate."

Mr. H—— bowed in acquiescence.

"On what day will you be prepared to place me in possession of the property?"

"Whenever you desire it."

"I desire it now," said the young man— "that is, just as soon as the proper legal papers can be executed. To-day I want five thousand dollars. Can I have it?"

Mr. H—— looked at the stripling, whose face already bore sad evidences of sensual indulgence and evil passion, and he hesitated to reply.

"Did you understand me, sir?" The manner of Charles Raynor was impatient.

"I understand you, Charles."

"Very well. Can I have the money to-day?"

"I do not wish to be intrusive, Charles; but as your late father's friend, and yours also, I will venture to ask as to the use you wish to make of this large sum of money?"

The young man drew himself up with an offended air, and said, with an effort to be dignified—

"I believe, sir, that I am fully competent to manage my own business. I am a man, and responsible to no one."

Mr. H—— bowed coldly, and replied,

"Come at one o'clock, sir, and I will be ready for you."

Charles drew out his watch and looked at it with an air of disappointment. It was just ten o'clock.

"At one, did you say?" A slight frown contracted his brows.

"Yes, sir; at one o'clock."

Charles bowed formally and withdrew. He had scarcely left the office when Mr. H——

took up his hat and went out in a hurried manner. His steps were directed to the house of Mrs. Raynor, with whom he asked an interview.

"Your son is of age to-day," he said, on meeting Mrs. Raynor.

"Yes; this is his twenty-first birthday," but in a tone that gave no sign of pleasure.

"He has just been to see me."

Mrs. Raynor looked, with a sober countenance, into the executor's face, but made no reply.

"He wishes to come into possession of his portion of his father's estate at once," said Mr. H——.

Mrs. Raynor's face grew troubled.

"He will squander it like water, I fear," she said.

"I fear as much," remarked the executor.

"Is there no way to keep it out of his hands?" asked the mother.

"I think not," was replied. "The provisions of the will are specific. I call, now, to mention that he wants five thousand dollars to-day, and is very urgent about the matter."

" Five thousand dollars !" exclaimed Mrs. Raynor, with a look of distress: "what possible use can he have for a sum of money like that ?"

"No good use, I fear," returned Mr. H——.

"Don't give it to him," said Mrs. Raynor, in a tone of much feeling.

" It will be an unpardonable offence," suggested the executor, "leading to a break between us, "and the destruction of all my influence over him in the future. Is it well to risk this consequence ?"

The face of Mrs. Raynor grew still more distressed.

" I see, I see," she answered, wringing her hands in a nervous, excited manner. "And if your influence is lost, there is no hope of him. He won't take a word of remonstrance or advice from me. Oh, I have wished a hundred times that his father had died poor."

" It would have been better for the boy, I'm sure," said Mr. H——. "But the question now is, shall I give him the money he demands? It is his by right, and if I withhold it now, it can only be for a short time."

"Do as you think best," replied Mrs. Raynor, tears flowing over her pale cheeks; "but, above all things, do not offend him. My only hope is in you. · When your control is lost, he is lost."

And the poor mother's frame shook with the wild strife of her feelings.

At one o'clock, to a minute, Charles Raynor called at the office of Mr. H——, who was grieved to see that he had been drinking.

"I will take that money," he said, with the air of a man who expected an immediate compliance with his wishes.

"It would suit me better to pay the amount to-morrow," replied Mr. H——, in a mild, conciliating tone. "Can't you possibly do without it until to-morrow?"

"Didn't I say that I wanted it to-day?" The young man showed some irritation.

"You did, Charles."

"Very well, sir; I meant just what I said.

You told me that you would be ready for me at one o'clock; and here I am."

Seeing that it would be in vain to parley with the young man, the executor took down his check-book, and filled out a check for five thousand dollars. He then wrote a receipt in due form, and required Charles to sign it. On handing him the check, he said,

"Your property is in stocks and real estate. The real estate is paying a good interest, and the stocks are among the safest in the market. I shall have to sell some of these stocks in order to realize the amount I now pay you."

"We'll talk about that another time," said Charles, interrupting Mr. H—— almost rudely, and turning away, he left the office.

Charles was not at home at tea-time. Ten, eleven, twelve, one o'clock came, and still he was absent. It was not a novel thing for him to be out late at night; indeed, he was rarely home before twelve or one o'clock. On this occasion Mrs. Raynor did not go to bed as usual. The fact that her son had demanded and probably received, five thousand dollars, caused her to feel great concern on his account, and she could not retire without seeing him. Long after every member of the household, except her son, was locked in slumber, she sat in anxious expectation, or walked the floor of her room with a troubled spirit; or stood, hushing her breath, at the window, listening for the sound of his well-known footsteps. It was one of the saddest nights she had ever spent. She felt that her son stood upon the brink of a wildly-rushing river, and in imminent danger of being swept away by the all-conquering flood. How feeble were her hands! Yet she felt that she must clutch after him, and hold him back from ruin, if that were possible.

It was nearly two o'clock when Charles came home. He entered with his night-key, ascended the stairs, and was passing the room of his mother, when the door opened and she stood before him..

"You are late to-night, my son," she said, in a kind, but grave voice.

He tried to pass her, but she laid her hand on his arm.

"Come into my room, Charles, I have something to say to you."

The young man followed his mother as she stepped back into her chamber. Drawing, him to a sofa, she sat down beside him, and looked earnestly into his face, the stronger light of her room enabling her to examine it closely. He did not meet her steady, searching glances, but looked past her, and tried to avert his countenance.

"Charles," Mrs. Raynor spoke in an impressive manner, "you were twenty-one to-day; but I am still your mother, and more interested in your welfare than any other human soul can possibly be. And now, may I take a mother's privilege, and ask where you have been to-day, and what you have done with the five thousand dollars you received from Mr. H——?"

The manner of Charles became instantly excited. He started from the sofa, and replied in an impatient voice.

"I do not care to be questioned in this style, mother! I had use for that sum of money, and have disposed of it in an honorable way."

"In that case, Charles, there is no reason why you should hesitate about satisfying me in regard to the way."

"Well, I don't choose to satisfy you," answered the young man, rather sharply, and showing still greater disturbance of manner; "and you might as well understand, once for all, that I don't mean to be catechised, or lectured, or interfered with. I'm old enough, it strikes me, to know my own business, and manage my own affairs."

Mrs. Raynor's face grew very pale, and she caught her breath several times in a choking way. For some moments the mother and son sat very still; then the latter arose, and without a word, passed from the chamber and went to his own apartment. As he left her room, the mother sank upon her knees, and bending down low upon the sofa, covered her face with her hands. An hour passed, and she still crouched there, like one who had fallen asleep; but her soul was too full of fear and pain for the opiate of slumber. Almost wildly she prayed for her son, until the very bitterness of her agony paralyzed her mind, and she sank into a dull, heartaching stupor, in which she took scarcely a note of the passing time. Morning found her lying across her bed, asleep.

When the mother and son met at breakfast time a barrier of reserve had been thrown up between them. Mrs. Raynor tried to cast it down, but Charles held it firmly in its place. He was a man, now, coming into possession of a fortune, which he meant to use as his own judgment and inclination dictated; he wished no interference from any one, not even from his mother. Mrs. Raynor tried to renew the conversation of the night before, but he affected not to understand her; and when she pressed the subject, he threw her off impatiently.

Thus it was that Charles Raynor started in life with his legacy of sixty thousand dollars. There were many who thought him a most-fortunate young man. Whether this was so or not, the sequel will prove.

———

"Twenty-five to-day," said Edward Strong, looking across the table at his mother and sister. It was evening, and they were sitting in a neatly furnished room. The mother and sister were sewing; Edward had been reading. The house they occupied was not that old, unattractive one from which we saw a funeral pass more than ten years ago, but a pleasant dwelling of larger size and ample accommodations.

Mrs. Strong raised her eyes, and looked fondly across the table at her son.

"How fast the years go by," she said. "Twenty-five! it seems but yesterday that you were a boy."

"I expect a visitor to-night," said Edward.

"Who?" was inquired.

"Mr. Campbell. As I was coming away this evening, he asked me where I lived, saying that he wished to have some conversation with me on a matter of business, and would call around."

Just then the bell rung. In a few moments word was brought to Edward that a gentleman was down stairs and wished to see him. It was Mr. Campbell.

"You have a very pleasant house, Edward," said his employer, as he took the young man's hand.

"Yes, sir ; we live very comfortably."

"How is your mother ?'

"In very good health, I thank you, sir."

There was a pause for a few moments, when Mr. Campbell said,

"I'm about making some changes in my business, which has increased so much of late, that its management has become very burdensome; and I must lay some of my cares on other and younger shoulders. Mr. Hewitt, my oldest salesman, has been with me since he was a boy, and has always shown himself true to my interests. You have also been with me since you were a boy, and have also shown yourself true to my interests. ' I now propose to unite you and Mr. Hewitt with me in business. I have already conversed with him, and now open the subject to you. He will have entire charge of the selling department; and you, if you enter the firm, of the manufacturing department. How does the matter strike you ?"

"And you're really in earnest, sir ?" Edward could hardly believe that he heard aright.

"Altogether in earnest," replied Mr. Campbell. "You can turn the matter over in your mind, and give me an answer at your earliest convenience."

"It needs no turning over, sir," was Edward's frankly spoken answer. "No deliberation. I say yes, without an instant's hesitation."

"Then the matter is settled. as to the fact," said Mr. Campbell; "and we have only to arrange the terms of copartnership. In a few days I will prepare a basis, when we can all meet and come to a full understanding."

When Mr. Campbell retired, and Edward

went up stairs, his mother and sister met him
with inquiring words, as well as inquiring
faces.

"What did Mr. Campbell want?" was
asked, with undisguised interest.

Edward took his place at the table, and
looking across it at his mother, said, while
his whole countenance lit up with a pleasure
that he could not suppress,

"As you would never for a moment imagine the good fortune that has come to my
door, I will tell you. Mr. Campbell has
offered me an interest in his business. 'I am
to be a partner."

"Oh, Edward!" exclaimed Mrs. Strong, her
face flushing with pride and joy. "This is
indeed good fortune. I could have asked
nothing better for you than this. But, what
to me is best of all, is the fact that you have
so honestly and patiently worked your way
to this position. That the good name your
father left you has never in a single instance
been tarnished; that our family heirloom is
as bright to-day, as when it passed into your

keeping. It was a richer legacy than gold, that may be scattered in a day; but this will endure forever."

————

, A different scene from this was passing in the house of Mrs. Raynor. That unhappy mother sat before her elegant rosewood escritoir, with her face buried in her hands, and an open letter lying beside her. She had been weeping; but the wild turbulence of her feelings had subsided, and she was now pondering sadly the contents of this letter, and trying to decide as to her duty. Slowly removing her hands, and lifting herself up, she took the letter, and read the few lines it contained, for the third time. It was dated New Orleans, and ran briefly thus,—

"DEAR MOTHER :

"Send me two hundred dollars immediately. I am sick, and out of funds, and I wish to get home. Don't fail, mother.

"Affectionately, your son,

"CHARLES."

"I sent him three hundred dollars a month ago," murmured Mrs. Raynor, as she held the letter before her eyes. "But there he is still; the money all wasted. If I send him more, it will be spent in dissipation, or at the gaming table, which has already swallowed up every dollar of his fortune."

At this moment the door opened, and the daughter of Mrs. Raynor came in. She held a letter in her hand.

"I have a letter from Charles, mother," she said, "and I want to talk with you about it.'

The eyes of the young girl were wet, and her countenance depressed and troubled.

"You a letter from Charles, Agnes!" Mrs. Raynor spoke in a tone of surprise. "When did you receive it?"

"To-day."

"What does he want?"

"Money."

"And from you?" said Mrs. Raynor, with increased surprise. "How much does he want?"

"A thousand dollars."

10

"A thousand dollars, Agnes!"

"Yes."

"For what purpose?"

"He wished me to keep the letter a secret from you; but, I fear I have already kept his secrets too long. From first to. last, I have sent him over ten thousand dollars."

"Why, Agnes!" The color that had come into the face of Mrs. Raynor, faded away, and she looked at her daughter with parted lips and brows contracted with pain. "Ten thousand dollars!" She repeated the words in blank astonishment. "Why did you keep this from me, my child?"

"Only because he desired it. I knew it was wrong."

"Does Mr. H—— know of this?"

"No. He often questioned me about my large drafts of money, but I did not give him any satisfaction."

"May I see your brother's letter?" asked Mrs. Raynor.

Agnes handed her mother the letter, who opened it and read,—

"DEAR SISTER:

"I must trespass once more on your generous kindness. Send me a thousand dollars without fail, immediately. I shall start, the moment I receive it, with a company of traders for Santa Fé. I have a warm friend in the company—a generous, noble fellow—with whom I am going into business, on arriving out. It is a rare opportunity, and I must not lose it, as I certainly shall, unless I receive from you the necessary funds for an outfit. Don't fail me now, dear Agnes! Every thing is at stake. A new life is opening before me —new prospects, new aims—a new sphere of action. I have seen my folly, and am resolved to recover all that I have lost. You have been a dear, good sister, and I will soon pay back all your many favors. Be sure to keep this from mother, and send the money without fail.   CHARLES."

Mrs. Raynor sat for some time, after reading this letter, without speaking or moving. then, looking up at her daughter, she said,

"How long is it since you sent Charles money?"

"About four weeks."

"How much did you send him then?"

"A thousand dollars."

"It can't be possible, Agnes!"

Mrs. Raynor looked bewildered. "I sent him three hundred dollars a month ago, and now he writes for two hundred more saying he is sick, and anxious to get home."

"Oh, mother!" ejaculated Agnes, clasping her hands together, and looking as pale, distressed, and bewildered as her mother. "Has he then become so lost to truth and honor?"

Mrs. Raynor made no answer, but her head sunk slowly on her bosom, and she sat for some time like one stupefied by a blow.

"What is to be done?" said Agnes, after a long silence.

"Nothing, until we have had a consultation with Mr. H——," replied the mother.

"Send him no more money," was the injunction of Mr. H—— when the matter was laid before him for consideration.

"But, what can I say to him?" inquired the anxious Mrs. Raynor. "He writes to me that he is sick, and asks for money to bring him home."

"And he writes to your daughter that he is going to Sante Fé," said Mr. H——. "The case is clear, that he is not sick. It is only a ruse to get money for evil purposes. If you comply with his wishes, you will waste your money, and do him an injury. Write to him plainly, as only a mother can and should write to her son. Let him know that you have discovered the double game he has been playing, and rebuke him severely for his dishonorable conduct. Depend upon it, madam, a resolute bearing on your part will be best for him. There should be no temporizing, no sign of weakness, no appearance of any thing but stern indignation at his falsehood and baseness. Pardon me for speaking so plainly."

"Mr. H—— is right," said Agnes, in a firm tone. "To send him money is like pouring it into a sieve. He has spent all his own fortune recklessly and riotously, and has commenced spending ours in the same way."

"The simple truth," remarked Mr. H——. "Take my advice, and either write to him in stern denial and rebuke, or remain wholly silent. Throw him upon his own resources, and let him earn his living as an honest man. Withhold from him the money he demands, and his false friends and evil associates will drop from him like leaves from a frost-touched tree. Such an abandonment will be a blessing. It would remove him in a degree from a charmed circle, or rather a whirling vortex, in whose centre is the pit of destruction. Necessity will force him to some useful employment, and in that lies our only hope."

Acting upon the suggestion of Mr. H——, Mrs. Raynor wrote a plain, rebuking letter to Charles, denying him any further advances of money. With anxious suspense, she waited for an answer to this letter, a thousand vague fears haunting her imagination. Her son was in a strange city, without money, without friends, and without skill in any useful work.

How then was he to sustain himself? What then could he do in the way of earning his own livelihood? Might not this abandonment drive him to desperation—to crime? A low shudder crept through the mother's heart, as she thought thus in regard to her son.

"I fear," she said to her daughter, as she sat with the one thought of Charles in her mind, "that we have done wrong in following so closely the advice of Mr. H——. If your brother is without money, and among strangers, what is he to do? How is he to help himself? What if he should do some desperate act? I shudder to think of it? The thought haunted me all through the night. I could not have slept an hour."

Just then the door-bell rung, and the mother and daughter listened in silence while a servant answered the summons. They did not hear the door shut again after it was opened, but the servant's steps came back along the hall, showing that a messenger was in waiting for an answer. He came in hold-

ing a letter in his hand, and said as he
handed it to Mrs. Raynor,

"A dispatch, ma'am, and the boy wishes
to know if there is an answer."

A deathlike paleness overspread the face
of Mrs. Raynor, as she caught eagerly the mis-
sive, and opened it with hands that trembled like aspen-leaves. There was a moment
of breathless suspense; then, with a cry of
anguish, Mrs. Raynor fell back in her chair,
lost to all present consciousness. As the dispatch fell from her hands, Agnes caught it
up and read it at a glance. Her brother was
dead. A pistol-shot had ended his feverish
life, though by whose hands the fatal ball had
reached his heart, the communication did not
say. But the sorrowful truth came too soon
—he had fallen by his own rash hand. Thus
the legacy of his father had proved to him a
curse, instead of a blessing. If he had received with it right principles, a carefully
trained mind, and habits of industry, his
wealth might have been the means of happiness to himself and usefulness to others. But

money without these was to him, as it is to all others like him, a power for evil instead of good.

Is there any question as to which of the two legacies was best; any question in the mind of the young man, who has the world all before him, with only his strong hands, clear head, and honest purposes, by which to reach its high places; any question in the mind of the father, whose love for his children prompts him to seek their highest good? There can be none!

VI.

CATCHING A SUNBEAM.

THE sun is always shining in the sky of our lives, and his beams coming down to gladden the earth. But into how few hearts do they find their way! The earth upon which our minds dwell, has, like the material earth, its dense forests, its deep, dim valleys, its dark caves and caverns, into which the sunlight rarely, if ever, comes. It would seem as if many people loved these gloomy shades, and hid themselves, of choice, away from the bright and beautiful sunshine. They carry shadows in their hearts and shadows on their faces. When they come into your presence it seems as if the air was suddenly darkened by a passing cloud.

Mr. Hickman was one of these men who walk for the most part, in dark valleys, or sit in dreary caverns. Rarely, if ever, on returning home, did he bring light into his dwelling. If there was merry laughter among the children on his entrance, their voices were hushed; if love's light beamed from the countenance of his wife, as she sported with her little ones, it faded away, giving place to a sober, thoughtful, half-troubled look. He always came home bringing a shadow with him, and sat, for the most part, in this shadow, through all the cheerless evenings.

Why was this? Was there a great trouble in the heart of Mr. Hickman? Had he passed through some depressing misfortune, or suffered some terrible affliction? No. It was as well with him as with most people—better than with a very large number. His business was prosperous, and every year he added many thousands of dollars to his rapidly accumulating fortune. But he was not a man possessing an orderly adjusted mind—was easily disturbed by trifles, and annoyed by incidents that should not have affected him any more than the buzzing of a fly. But the real cause lay deeper and more hidden, grounded in an inordinate selfishness, that robbed him of the pleasure which might have attended success, through envy of others' good fortune. He was jealous of his compeers in business, and always experienced a disagreeable sensation when he heard them spoken of as successful. No wonder that sunlight could not find its way into his heart. Envy and ill-will, burn in what heart they may, always send up a black smoke that obscures the heavens. The sun is there, shining as brightly as ever, but his rays cannot penetrate this cloud of passion. No day passed in which something did not occur to disturb or cloud the mind of Mr. Hickman; and so, evening after evening he came home, bringing with him shadow instead of sunlight. Oh, what a desecration of home was this! of home, where the heart's sunlight should ever dwell, and a heart-warmth pervade all the sweet atmosphere. Nothing of external good was denied by Mr. Hickman to his family. They had all of happiness that money could buy. Yet how far from happiness were his wife and children. They were drooping for sunshine—the sunshine of smiles, and pleasant words, and joyous laughter. But these came not from Mr. Hickman. He sat among them grim and gloomy, for the most part, like some sombre heathen divinity —half dreaded, half propitiated.

Mr. Hickman was not so stolid but that he saw in this the existence of a wrong. He loved his wife and children, desired their good, and was ready to make almost any sacrifice for them that he knew how to make. Even as he sat moodily in his home, conscious that his presence rested like a nightmare on the spirits of his wife and children, he would say to himself—

"This is not right. I should bring home pleasant words and cheerful smiles."

Yet almost as he said this would his thought go back to some incident of the day, which mere selfishness gave power to disturb his feelings, and he would go off again into a brooding state of mind, out of which he had not resolution enough to lift himself. Often it happened that his children sought, in the outgushing gladness of their hearts, to break the spell that was on him—but almost always he repulsed them—sometimes coldly, sometimes fretfully, and sometimes in sudden anger—so that, at last, they rarely came near or spoke to him, as he sat through his silent evenings.

"Wrong, all wrong," Mr. Hickman often said to himself, as the shadow fell darker on his home. But a knowledge of the evil did not bring a knowledge of the cure, or, rather, that self-conquest which must precede a cure. He must let the sunshine come into his own heart ere he could pour forth its rays on other hearts. He must come out of the dense forests, and gloomy valleys, and dusky caverns, into the clear sunshine; but how was he to come out? Who was to lead him forth?

One day, as Mr. Hickman sat in his counting-room conversing with a gentleman, a lad

CATCHING A SUNBEAM. 159

came in from the store to ask him some question about business. Mr. Hickman replied in a curt way, and the lad went out.

"What is that boy's name?" asked the gentleman.

"Frank Edwards," was replied.

"I thought so. He's a fine boy. How long has he been with you?"

"About three months."

"Does he give satisfaction?"

"Yes."

"I'm pleased to hear it. His mother lives in our neighborhood, and my wife has taken considerable interest in her. She is very poor and in feeble health. She maintains herself, by sewing; but that kind of exhausting toil is wasting her life rapidly. Frank is her only child, and the only one to whom she can look for any help. I am glad you like him."

Nothing more was said on the subject, but it did not pass from the mind of Mr. Hickman. He had taken the lad a few months before on trial. and it was understood that if he gave satisfaction, he was to be put on wages after six months.

"The boy is faithful, intelligent and active," said Mr. Hickman, speaking to himself. "If it is so with his mother, he must be put on wages now."

This conclusion in the mind of Mr. Hickman was attended with a sense of pleasure. His heart had opened just a little, and two or three sunbeams, with their light and warmth, had gone down into it.

"What shall I pay him for his services?" said Mr. Hickman to himself, still dwelling on the subject.

"There are plenty of lads to be obtained at a couple of dollars a week, for the first one or two years; or even for nothing, in consideration of the opportunity for learning a good business in a good house. But Frank's case is peculiar, and must be considered by itself. There is a question of humanity involved. His mother is poor and sick, and she has no hope but in him. Let me see; shall I make it three dollars a week? That will help them considerably. But, dear me! three dollars will hardly pay for Frank's eating. I must do something better than that. Say four dollars."

Mr. Hickman dropped his head a little, and sat turning the matter over in his mind. He had once been a poor boy, with a mother in feeble health; and he remembered how hard it was for him to get along—how many privations his mother had to endure; and yet their income was nearly double the amount he thought of giving Frank. Mr. Hickman had always loved his mother, and this memory of her softened his feelings still more toward the poor widow, for whom an appeal had come to him so unexpectedly.

"Frank is an unusually bright boy," said Mr. Hickman. "He has an aptness for business; is prompt and faithful. I can afford to make his salary liberal—for a boy it shall be liberal. I'll pay him six dollars now, and if he goes on improving as fast as he has done so far, it will not be long before I can make it better for him."

11

Mr. Hickman arose, and going to the counting-room door, called the lad, who came in immediately.

"How do you like our business, Frank?" asked Mr. Hickman, in a kind way.

"Very well, sir," replied the boy, promptly.

"And you would like to remain?"

"Yes, sir, if I give satisfaction."

"You have done very well, so far," replied Mr. Hickman; "so well, that I have concluded to put you on wages now, instead of waiting until the six months of trial have expired."

The boy started, and a quick flush of surprise and pleasure went over his face.

"I did not expect it, sir," he said, gratefully. "You are very good."

"Your mother is not well, I hear," said Mr. Hickman.

Frank's eyes glistened as he answered, "No, sir; she has been sick for a good while; and I'm so glad to be put on wages, for now I can help her."

"Will you give all your wages to your mother?"

"Oh, yes indeed, sir; every cent, if it was ten dollars a week."

"I see you're a good boy, Frank," said Mr. Hickman, his heart still softening, "and your wages shall be six dollars."

The boy struck his hands together with sudden joy, exclaiming,

"Oh, mother will be so glad!—so glad!"

As he went back into the store, Mr. Hickman sat quietly in his chair, feeling happier than he had been for a long time. When the sun went down, and Frank came in to shut the windows of the counting-room, Mr. Hickman handed him a sealed envelope, saying,

"Take this to your mother. It contains thirty-six dollars, as your wages, at three dollars a week for twelve weeks, the time you have been in my store. Tell your mother that you have been a good, industrious boy, and have earned the money."

Frank took the little package in silence; his feelings were so much overcome by this additional good fortune, that he could not speak his thanks. But his eyes told what was in his heart, and Mr. Hickman understood them.

There are many ways to catch sunbeams, if we would only set traps for them. Nay, there is no occasion to go to that trouble. The air is full of sunbeams, and we have only to open the doors and windows of our hearts, and they will enter in countless multitudes. But the doors and windows of most people's hearts are shut and barred as was the heart of Mr. Hickman. How are they to be opened? Just as the doors and windows of his heart were opened—by kindness to others.

When Mr. Hickman took his way homeward, his step was lighter and his feelings more buoyant than they had been for a long time. Though conscious of this, and of the sense of pleasure that was new to him, his thought did not go directly to the cause. Not that he had forgotten Frank and his sick mother; or the glad face that looked into his when he told the boy of his generous decision in his favor; all this was present to him, though he had not yet connected the kind act and the pleasant feelings in his consciousness as cause and effect.

There were no sounds of pattering feet on the stairs as Mr. Hickman came in. Time was when his first step in the passage awoke the echoes with laughing voices and the rain of eager footfalls. But, that time had passed long ago. The father came home so often in a cold, repellent mood, that his children had ceased to be glad at his return, and no longer bounded to meet him. Sitting on the stairs were a little boy and girl, of the ages of five and six years. As he advanced along the passage, they neither stirred, nor spoke, nor smiled, though their eyes were fixed on his face. Mr. Hickman stood still when he came near to where they were sitting, and looked at them with a new feeling of tenderness in his heart. He held out a hand to each, and each laid a hand in his, but with an air of doubt as to whether this condescension on the part of their father were to be accepted as a token of love. A moment he stood holding their hands, then stooping, he drew an arm around each and lifted them to his breast.

"Hasn't Edie a kiss for papa?" said Mr. Hickman, with so much warmth in his voice, that the little girl now understood that all was earnest.

"Yes, a hundred kisses!" answered Edie, flinging her arms around her father's neck, and kissing him over and over again in childish fondness.

At the head of the first landing, opened the sitting-room. Into this Mr. Hickman came with the two children in his arms; both of them hugging and kissing him in a wild, happy way:

"Bless me! what's the meaning of all this?" exclaimed Mrs. Hickman, rising and coming forward, her face a-glow with sudden pleasure at a sight and sounds so new, yet all welcome to her heart.

"These little rogues are hugging and kissing the very breath away from me," said Mr.

"Mr. Hickman came with the two children in his arms," etc.

Hickman, laughing and struggling with the children.

"He asked me for one kiss," cried Edie, "and I'm going to give him a hundred."

Mr. Hickman sat down with a child on each knee, and Mrs. Hickman came and stood by him, with a hand resting on his shoulder.

"Oh, you must kiss him too," said Edie, looking up at her mother.

Mrs. Hickman did not wait for a second invitation.

The old pleasant face of her husband was again before her, and her heart was leaping with the old loving impulses. She bent down and laid a warm kiss on his lips, which he felt as a sweet glow through all his being.

That was an evening long to be remembered in the household of Mr. Hickman. He had caught a sunbeam and brought it home with him, and light and warmth were all around them. All were happy, and Mr. Hickman the happiest of them all, for he had the sweet consciousness in his heart of having made another and humbler home than this happy also.

VII.

DIDN'T LIKE HIS WIFE.

OUR minister is a favorite in the congregation; he's so approachable, so kind, so pleasant and sympathizing! Everybody likes him—the young and the old, the rich and the poor. And he's such an eloquent preacher! In all his private relations, as well as in his public ministries, he seems about as near perfection as can be hoped for on this earth. Now, that is saying a great deal for our minister.

But there is no unmixed good. in this world. We are not permitted to enjoy our minister without the accompaniment of some unpleasant drawback. Mr. Elmore has a wife, and a minister's wife, it is well known, is not usually perfect in the eyes of the congregation. There was no exception to the rule in our case. Mrs. Elmore was no favor-

ite. What the real trouble was I did not
know from personal observation. But no
one seemed to have a friendly feeling toward
her. When I say no one, I refer to the ladies
of our congregation. When Mr. Elmore was
the subject of conversation, you would be
almost certain to hear the remark—"Ah, if it
wasn't for his wife."

Or—"What a pity Mrs. Elmore isn't the
right kind of a woman!"

Or—"Isn't it a shame that he has a wife so
poorly fitted for her position!"

So the changes rang. Mr. Elmore had
been our minister for over a year, and during
that time very little had been seen of his wife
in a social way. The ladies of the congregation had called upon her, and she had received them kindly and politely, but with a
certain distance in her manner that repelled
rather than attracted. In every case she
returned these calls, but when repeated, failed in that prompt reciprocation which her
visitors expected. There are, in all congregations, certain active, patronizing ladies, who

like to manage things, to be deferred to, and to make their influence felt on all around them. The wife of our previous minister, a weak and facile woman, had been entirely in their hands, and was, of course, a great favorite. But Mrs. Elmore was a different character altogether. You saw by the poise of her head—by the steadiness of her clear, dark blue eyes—and by the firmness of her delicate mouth, that she was a woman of independent thought, purpose, and self-reliance. Polite and kind in her intercourse with the congregation, there was, withal, a coldness of manner that held you at a certain distance, as surely as if a barrier had been interposed.

It was a serious trouble with certain ladies of the congregation, this peculiarity in the minister's wife. How he could ever have married a woman of her temperament was regarded as a mystery. He so genial—she so cold; he so approachable by every one—she so constrained; he all alive for the church— and she seemingly indifferent to every thing but her own family. If she had been the lawyer's wife, or the doctor's wife, or the wife of a merchant, she might have been as distant and exclusive as she pleased; but for the minister's wife! O dear! it was terrible!

I had heard so much said about Mrs. Elmore, that, without having met her familiarly, or knowing any thing about her from personal observation, I took for granted the general impression as true.

Last week one of my lady friends, a member of Mr. Elmore's congregation, called in to see me. I asked her to take off her bonnet and sit for the afternoon. But she said—

"No; I have called for you to go with me to Mrs. Elmore's."

"I have not been in the habit of visiting her," was my answer.

"No matter," was replied, "she's our minister's wife, and it's your privilege to call on her."

"It might not be agreeable," I suggested; "you know she is peculiar."

"Not agreeable to the minister's wife to

have a lady of the congregation call on her!"
and my friend put on an air of surprise.

"She's only a woman, after all," I remarked, "and may have her likes and dislikes,
her peculiarities and preferences, as well as
other people. And I'm sure that I have no
desire to intrude upon her."

"Intrusion! How you talk! An intrusion to call on our minister's wife! Well,
that sounds beautiful, don't it? I wouldn't
say that again. Come, put on your bonnet. I
want your company and am going to have it."

I made no further objection, and went with
my lady friend to call on Mrs. Elmore. We
sent up our names, and were shown into her
neat little parlor, where we sat nearly five
minutes before she came down.

"She takes her own time," remarked my
companion.

If the tone of voice in which this was said
had been translated into a sentence it would
have read thus—

"She's mighty independent for a minister's
wife."

I did not like the manner, nor the remark of my friend, and so kept silent. Soon, there was a light step on the stairs, the rustle of garments near the door, and then Mrs. Elmore entered the room where we were sitting. She received us kindly, but not with wordy expressions of pleasure. There was a mild, soft light in her eyes, and a pleasant smile on her delicately arching lips. We entered into conversation, which was a little constrained on her part; but whether this was from coldness or diffidence I could not decide. I think she did not, from some cause, feel entirely at her ease. A remark in the conversation gave my companion the opportunity of saying what I think she had come to say.

"That leads me to suggest, Mrs. Elmore, that, as our minister's wife, you hold yourself rather too far at a distance. You will pardon me for saying this, but as it is right that you should know how we feel on this subject, I have taken the liberty of being frank with you. Of course, I mean no offence, and I am sure you will not be hurt at an intimation given in all kindness."

I looked for a flash from Mrs. Elmore's clear bright eyes, for red spots on her cheeks, for 'a quick curving of her flexible lips— but none of these signs of feeling were apparent. Calmly she looked into the face of her monitor, and when the above sentence was completed, answered in a quiet tone of voice—

"I thank you for having spoken so plainly. Of course, I am not offended. But I regret to learn that any one has found cause of complaint against me. I have not meant to be cold or distant, but my home-duties are many and various, and take most of my time and thoughts."

"But, my dear madam," was answered to this, with some warmth, "you forget that for a woman in your position there are duties beyond the home circle which may not be omitted."

"In my position?" Mrs. Elmore's calm eyes rested in the face of my companion with a look of inquiry. "I am not sure that I understand you."

"You are the wife of our minister."

"I am aware of that." I thought I saw a twinkle in Mrs. Elmore's eyes.

"Well, ma'am, doesn't that involve some duties beyond the narrow circle of home?"

"No more than the fact of your being a merchant's wife involves you in obligations that reach beyond the circle of your home. My husband is your minister, and, as such, you have claims upon him. I think he is doing his duty earnestly and conscientiously. I am his wife and the mother of his children, and, as such, I too am trying to do my duty earnestly and conscientiously. There are immortal souls committed to my care, and I am endeavoring to train them up for heaven."

"I think you misapprehend your relation to the church," was replied to this, but not in the confident manner in which the lady had at first spoken.

"I have no relation to the church in any way different from yours, or that of other

ladies in the congregation," said Mrs. Elmore, with a decision of tone that showed her
to be in earnest.

"But you forget, madam, that you are the
minister's wife."

"Not for a moment. I am the minister's
wife, but not the minister. He is a servant
of the congregation, but I am not!"

I glanced toward my friend, and saw that
she looked bewildered and at fault. I think
some new ideas were coming into her mind.

"Then, if I understand you," she said,
"you are in no way interested in the spiritual
welfare of your husband's congregation?"

"On the contrary," replied Mrs. Elmore,
"I feel deeply interested. And I also feel
interested in the spiritual welfare of other
congregations. But I am only a wife and
mother, and my chief duties are at home. If,
time permitting, I can help in any good work
outside of my home, I will put my hand to it
cheerfully. But, home obligations are first
with me. It is my husband's duty to minister in spiritual things—not mine. He engaged

to preach for you, to administer the ordinances of the church, and to do faithfully all things required by his office. So far as I know, he gives satisfaction."

"O, dear—yes, indeed, *he* gives satisfaction!" was replied to this. "Nobody has a word to say against *him*."

A smile of genuine pleasure lit up the face of Mrs. Elmore. She sat very still for a few moments, and then, with the manner of one who had drawn back her thoughts from something agreeable, she said,

"It is very pleasant for me to hear such . testimony in regard to my husband. No one knows so well as I do how deeply his heart is in his work."

"And if you would only hold up his hands," suggested my friend.

"Help him to preach, do you mean?"

"Oh, no—no!" was ejaculated. "I don't mean that, of course." The warm blood mounted to the very forehead of my lady monitor.

Mrs. Elmore smiled briefly, and as the light
12

faded from her countenance, said, in her grave, impressive way.

"I trust we are beginning to understand each other. But I think a word or two more is required to make my position clear. In arranging for my husband's services, no stipulation was made in regard to mine. If the congregation expected services from me, the fact should have been stated. Then I would have communicated my view in the case, and informed the congregation that I had neither time nor taste for public duties. If this had not been satisfactory, the proposition to my husband could have been withdrawn. As it is, I stand unpledged beyond any lady in the parish; and what is more, shall remain unpledged. I claim no privileges, no rights, no superiority; I am only a woman, a wife, and a mother—your sister and your equal—and as such I ask your sympathy, your kindness, and your fellowship. If there are ladies in the congregation who have the time, the inclination, and the ability to engage in the more public uses to be found in all religious societies, let them, by all means, take the precedence. They will have their reward in just the degree that they act from purified Christian motives. As for me, my chief duties, as I have said before, lie at home, and, God being my helper, I will faithfully do them."

"Right, Mrs. Elmore, right!" said I, speaking for the first time, but with a warmth that showed my earnestness. "You have stated the case exactly. When we engaged your husband's services, nothing was stipulated, as you have said, in regard to yours, and I now see that no more can be justly required of you than of any other lady in the congregation. I give you my hand as an equal and a sister, and thank you for putting my mind right on a subject that has always been a little confused."

"She knows how to take her own part," said my companion, as we walked away from the house of our minister. Her manner was a little crest-fallen.

"She has right and common sense on her

side," I answered, "and if we had a few more such minister's wives in our congregations, they would teach the people some lessons needful to be learned."

I was very favorably impressed with Mrs. Elmore on the occasion of this visit, and shall call to see her again right early. To think how much hard talk and uncharitable judgment there has been in regard to her; and all because, as a woman of good sense and clear perceptions, she understood her duty in her own way, and, as she understood it, performed it to the letter. I shall take good care to let her view of the case be known. She will rise at once in the estimation of all whose good opinion is worth having. We are done with complaints about our minister's wife, I trust. She has defined her position so clearly, that none but the most stupid or self-willed can fail to see where she stands.

VIII.

THE DISCIPLINE OF MISFORTUNE.

ADELE LEHMAN had reached the ripe age of eighteen, and began to feel womanly and self-important. And why not self-important? Was not her father, Andrew Lehman, the richest man in Ashville? Tired of school, she had persuaded her too yielding parents to let her education close as full and complete; and now she had nothing to do but play the lady, and wait for a lover. As a school-girl, Adele had been on free and easy terms with most of her companions; her likes and dislikes being grounded in peculiarity of character, and not in external condition. She had, of course, her closer intimacies, as all girls have, and, like most girls, had one particular friend who shared her secret thoughts. This was Flora Lee, the daughter of Doctor Lee, whose pleasant little dwelling stood not very far away from Mr. Lehman's elegant mansion.

Flora was a kind, gentle, disinterested girl, with qualities that always attract. She was a favorite with all in her class, but most intimate with Adele Lehman. The two girls left school within a few months of each other— Adele to pass the time in comparative idleness, and Flora to join her mother in home duties, and lighten the burdens under which her weak shoulders were bending.

It was now that Adele's thoughts began to take a new range, and her mind to be filled with ideas of her own importance. The associations of the past were for the past time— mere school-girl intimacies that must close. Her sphere in life was different from that of nearly all her old companions. She must take one place in society, they another. Adele went home three months before Flora's term closed. During that interval, Flora wrote two or three warm letters to her friend, but received only one answer in return, and that filling just two pages of small note-paper, and so guardedly worded that its formal sentences chilled her feelings like a winter wind. But she had no suspicion of the true cause of this seeming coldness. Two days after her return home, and before she had time to call upon Adele, she met her in the street. Adele was in company with a richly-dressed young lady, to her a stranger. As they approached, Flora paused to speak, her face lit up with smiles; but Adele passed quickly as if she had not seen her.

"I thought that girl was going to speak to you," said the companion of Adele.

"I thought so myself," was replied, with a toss of the head and a curl of the lip, "but I didn't choose to give her the opportunity."

"Who is she?"

"Oh, a mere school-girl acquaintance, that must, of necessity, be dropped. She's one of the ordinary kind, but while we formed part of the same household circle, she had to be tolerated. Now things are changed. I have returned to my sphere in life, and she has re turned to hers. We are acquaintances no longer. I am sorry to hurt her feelings, but it can't be helped. She should have known her place better."

Poor Flora! She was hurt severely by this cut direct. She had been sincerely attached to Adele, and looked forward to meeting her with lively pleasure. Of their difference in worldly condition she had never thought. She loved Adele for herself alone. After returning home and thinking over the matter, it seemed so impossible for her late friend to pass her unnoticed, that she tried to persuade herself that Adele had not really observed her. But all doubt was removed a few days after, when she met her again. This time Adele was alone. The meeting was so sudden and unexpected that there was no chance to appear unconscious of the proximi- • ty of Flora. A cold, stiff nod was the only response given to her friend's warm greeting. Wounded pride sent the hot blood to Flora's cheeks, and wounded affection filled her eyes with tears.

And so the friends parted, both in an unhappy state of mind, but Adele really the un-

happiest of the two, for selfish pride was not
yet strong enough to crush out the better impulses of her nature. Still, what she had
done had been from a deliberate purpose, and
she had no thought of receding. Of the two
young ladies, Flora was the superior in almost
every thing. She had a finer face and a finer
form than Adele. She had also a better mind
and a better education. In the way of accom-
plishments there was only one thing in which
she was excelled by Adele. The latter had a
fine musical taste, which had been largely cul-
tivated, while Flora had scarcely any talent in
that direction, and, after taking a few lessons,
had given up the study of music entirely.
The refined, educated circle of Ashville was
not large enough to be very exclusive, and
there were very few who thought of passing
by the intelligent Dr. Lee and his wife.
Within a year after Flora's return from
school, she began to go into company with
her father and mother, and soon became a favorite with almost every one. The beauty
and refinement of her face, the pleasant frank-

ness of her manner, the good feeling and intelligence she uniformly displayed, won for her a place in the hearts of nearly all who met her. As just said, the refined and educated circle of Ashville was not very large, and as Flora Lee was not excluded therefrom, Adele Lehman often met her on a plane of social equality. But after the cruel repulse which Flora had received, and the estrangement which followed, there was no desire on her part to renew the acquaintance with the purse-proud young lady; and shame united with pride to keep Adele aloof from her. And so they stood apart as strangers.

Dr. Lee was a man skilled in his profession, and his practice steadily increased from year to year. He was poor when he came to Ashville, but his worldly affairs had improved from the beginning. As money came in beyond his needs, he made careful investments, and these turning out favorably in almost every instance, he was now worth quite a handsome little property, which was entirely unencumbered. Though not called a rich man, there were few in Ashville whose affairs were in so easy and comfortable a condition. But neither Dr. Lee nor his family were ostentatious in their feelings, and so continued to occupy the modest home which industry and economy had first secured to them.

Mr. Lehman was a man of altogether a different spirit. He was ambitious for large accumulations. Through sharp business transactions, and bold, but fortunate speculations, he had acquired great wealth. But speculation is only another name for gambling, and one day the cards turned adversely for Mr. Lehman, and he lost his game. The stake had been a large one, and if he had won he would have doubled his fortune; but "luck," as they say, was against him. He was rich in the morning, but poor as any man in Ashville when the sun went down at night. A brave man was Mr. Lehman when the day was broad and bright around him, and he could see his vantage-ground; but he was a weak, bewildered coward in storm and darkness; and now the shadows of an Egyptian night were upon him. ˙ The shock prostrated him to the earth. Courage, hope, effort, all were gone. He tottered about like a man who felt the ground shaking beneath him—weak, frightened, and nerveless.

It does not take long for the external condition of a man so hopelessly ruined as Mr. Lehman, to change. In a few months after the disaster we find the humiliated family shrinking together in a small house, far humbler in appéarance than the one occupied by the unostentatious Dr. Lee, without means and without income. And to make all sadder and more hopeless, a stroke of paralysis reduced Mr. Lehman to a condition of helplessness. What was now to be done? With all her pride, weakness, and vanity, Adele Lehman had loved her father most tenderly. He had been a fond and indulgent parent, too much so for her own good. But indulgence had tended rather to strengthen, than to weaken her love. In the first step downward she was overwhelmed with mortification. The anguish of crushed pride seemed

more than she could bear; and she shrank
within the narrow walls that enclosed them
in their new home, feeling so helpless and dis-
graced that she wished to die. But the added
blow which made her father a feeble invalid,
startled her mind with a new thought. Who
were they to lean upon now that he was
stricken down? What hand was to sustain
them? From whence was to come their sup-
port? Her mother was in feeble health, and
her sisters but little children. She alone had
strength and skill, and love sent her thought
out in eager questioning. "What can I do?"
Ah! how long she searched for an answer!
But it came. She was skilled in music, and
competent to teach. But oh! with what an
irrepressible aversion did she turn from the
thought of becoming a music-teacher—the
patient toiling instructor of those, down upon
whom she had looked, only a few months ago,
as mean and inferior! But no help came in
their need—no way opened before them.

Few friends are left to a family so utterly
ruined as that of Mr. Lehman. Many who

pity and sympathize, hesitate about visiting them in their altered circumstances, lest their presence should prove disagreeable, as a reminder of the height from which they had fallen ; while the more heartless and worldly, having nothing to gain by association, push them out from the circle of their friends. And now it is that some humble acquaintances of their better days, whose familiarity was rather tolerated than desired, draw nearer to them with that true interest, which asks, "How can we help you ?"

It happened not long after the Lehmans had removed to their new home, that a friend of this class sat in earnest talk with Adele and her mother. The pressure of impending want had made them communicative, and this friend had come earnestly into their councils.

"There is only one thing which I can do," said Adele, her eyes filling with tears when she thought of the great trial and humiliation that lay before her. "I understand music, and feel competent to give instruction."

"A good teacher is wanted in Ashville,"

replied the friend, "and I am sure that after you become known as such, there will be no lack of scholars. The difficulty lies in getting a start. Your former social position will be just so much against you in the beginning. For many in the circle where you moved, and many in the one below it, will hesitate about asking your services; some from delicacy, some from prejudice, and some from the belief that, while you may be a good performer, you can have no skill as a teacher. Much will depend on a right commencement. Let me see. Ah! I think I have it. It was only last week that I was talking to Mrs. Lee about a music-teacher. She said, their eldest daughter, Flora, had no musical taste whatever, but that her two younger sisters showed decided talent, and that they had been talking for some time about placing them in the hands of a teacher. Now you couldn't have a better beginning. If you can give satisfaction there, all the rest will be plain. Dr. Lee has a large practice in our best families. Both he and his wife are much esteemed. With their influence, you will have as many pupils as you want. Go and see Mrs. Lee at once; she is a true, motherly woman, and will be interested in your case. Her daughter Flora is a charming girl; and if you have never made her acquaintance, you will now have the opportunity, I think, of securing a friend that is worthy of the name."

Poor Adele! Had it come to this? Was there no other way for her but through this valley of humiliation? The friend went home, and the unhappy girl retired to her chamber to think over the suggestion alone. How vividly did the past come up before her! She was back in her school-girl days; in that pleasant time when she called Flora Lee her best and dearest friend. Then she remembered the cold heartlessness with which she had turned from this friend; not because Flora was less worthy, but because false pride had come between them. And could she go to her now, in her great extremity? In her wild struggle with pride she felt that death would be easier than this.

But the wolf was at their door, and there was no help but in her. For three days a bitter strife went on in her mind, and then, sad, humbled, and fearful of the result, she turned her hesitating steps toward the dwelling of Dr. Lee. Was it possible for Mrs. Lee to forgive the indignity she had placed upon her daughter? How could she meet Flora and look her in the face, with the memory of that past time as vividly in her thoughts as if it had occurred but yesterday? How she despised herself for that mean pride which had prompted to so unworthy an action! This was her state of mind when she arrived at Dr. Lee's house and timidly rang the bell. A few moments she stood with fluttering heart, when the door opened, and she looked into the face of Flora Lee. Her own face was pale, her lips quivered; she tried to speak, but found no utterance.

"Adele Lehman!" exclaimed Flora, in a voice of surprise, at the same time offering her hand. There was neither resentment nor coldness in her manner, but a tone of warmth

13

and sympathy that touched the heart of
Adele, and made her eyes brimming with
tears.

"Is your mother at home?" inquired Adele,
in a faltering voice.

"She is. Do you wish to see her?"

"If you please."

There was something in the subdued, humble manner of Adele, that touched the heart
of, Flora. She knew of the misfortune that
had overwhelmed her family; of the prostra-
ting, almost hopeless illness of her father;
and had heard with pain, that they were reduced in circumstances, almost to the verge
of want. The sight of Adele's pale, suffering
face, revived the old-time affection in her
heart, and she drew an arm around her waist
and led her in to her mother. Mrs. Lee received her with great kindness, and as soon
as Adele was composed enough to speak,
listened with much interest to the brief story
she told of their necessities, and the duty
which devolved upon her. Flora entered
warmly into her feelings; spoke encoura-

gingly; praised her skill in music, and predicted certain success.

"You can depend on two scholars here," said Mrs. Lee, without hesitation, "and I think that I can promise you half a dozen more in a week. If not, the fault will not lie at my door. You are a brave, good girl, Adele; you deserve success, and it will come."

A reception like this had not been dreamed of by the poor girl. Her own mind had been so warped by foolish pride and false ideas, that she could not imagine any thing so forgiving, so generous, and so disinterested.

"Shall we not be friends again?" said Flora, as she moved with Adele toward the door, when the visit was ended.

"Friends?" Adele looked at Flora in surprise.

"Yes; we were friends once, why shall we not be so again?"

"I am not worthy to be called by the name," said Adele, completely broken down.

"More worthy than ever," replied Flora;

"an enemy came between us, but his power is gone."

As Adele Lehman turned her feet away from the dwelling of Dr. Lee, there was the beginning of a new life in her soul. She had gone trembling and fearful; scarcely hoping for any thing but repulse, or if not repulse, coldness, reserve, and scarcely-hidden contempt. There were lions in her way, and only the courage of despair had given her strength to face the evil that loomed up before her. But, like Christian's lions at the Beautiful gate, they were chained, and she passed them harmless.

This visit to Mrs. Lee and Flora, was like a new revelation to Adele Lehman, passing, for a time, her comprehension But as she became an earnest worker, going through her daily duties under the impulse of filial and fraternal love, her sight grew clearer, and she comprehended the wide difference between selfish pride and genuine goodness of heart.

Mrs. Lee was no mere lip-friend. She meant all that she said, and was as good as her word. Through her influence, a number of scholars were immediately obtained, and Adele commenced her new life a hopeful, patient toiler, sustained in her work by the love she bore the helpless ones at home. And her weak arm sustained them. Bravely she battled with the wolf, and kept the hungry destroyer from their door. And was she not better for this great worldly misfortune; for this deep humiliation through which she had to pass; this bowing of pride to the very dust? Yes, it was painful, but salutary; and there came a time, in her after-life, when she lifted her heart upward, and thanked God for humiliation and misfortune, for they had made her what she otherwise would not have been, a true woman.

IX.

WORK AND WORRY.

I HAVE two neighbors who interest me considerably. One is a poor woman with four children, and wholly dependent on her labor for food and clothing. The other is the wife of a citizen, comfortably well off, and has two servants to do the work of her household. It is about two years since I first commenced observing them, and both have failed considerably in that time. If the work of exhaustion continues as rapidly as it has been going on for the last twelve months, it will only take a year or two more to complete their life-histories. My poor neighbor I think will hold out longest, as the disease from which she is suffering does not break down the constitution so quickly as the one that has robbed my other neighbor's cheeks of their bloom, and her step of its lightness.

Yesterday I called in to see Mrs. M——. I found her standing over a washing-tub, with a pale, weary face. It was three o'clock in the afternoon, and, from the quantity and condition of her work, it was plain that she had yet two hours of exhausting labor before her.

"Always hard at work, Mrs. M——," said I.

"Yes," she answered, with a faint smile. "I and Work are old friends."

"Work," I remarked, "is a friend that sticks to some people closer even than a brother."

"You may well say that," was her reply to this, with an amused expression on her thin face. "I am Work's favorite sister."

I smiled in return, and said:

"You manage to keep cheerful with it all, Mrs. M——."

"Not always cheerful, and never very sad. I sing at my work sometimes, and that makes it lighter."

I glanced around the room. To my eyes every thing wore a cheerless aspect. Two neglected children were playing on the floor. Perhaps I ought not to say neglected, for their faces were clean, and their clothes not in a very bad condition. Yet it was plain to see that the mother's hands were too full of work to care for them properly.

"Singing," said I, "is better than sighing. I am glad you have heart enough to sing at your work."

"Why shouldn't I? Everybody has to work; some harder than others, it is true; but it all goes in the lifetime. I am too thankful to get work, to sit down and cry over it."

"And so you sing to make it lighter?"

"Yes," she answered, in a quiet way.

"Your health is not very good?" said I.

"Not so good as it was a year ago. I tire more quickly, and suffer oftener with bad headaches. Of late, I have been a good deal troubled with a pain in my side. But I try not to think of it. Thinking about pains and troubles, you know, always makes them worse."

"I know some people," said I, "who would be happier than they are, if they had a few grains of your philosophy."

"Our minister says that we make, for the most part, our world of happiness or misery. And I believe him. Why, if I gave way to gloomy thoughts, I could make myself wretched all the day long. But what would be the use of that? It wouldn't lighten my work any, but make it heavier; and, dear above knows, it is heavy enough now! Some one has said, that worry kills quicker than work. It is as much as I can do to keep up under the burden of work; add worry, and I would break down in a week. I don't trouble myself a great deal about what I can't help, and try to act on the precept of the good Book which says, 'Take no thought for the morrow.' The truth is, it's as much as I can do to take thought for each day as it comes along. We only have a day at a time, you know; and it's my belief, that if we improve our to-days rightly, God will take care of our to-morrows.'"

Mrs. M—— bent down over her washing-tub, and resumed her work, adding, as she did so—

"But we must improve our nows as well as our to-days. .I've got full two hours' work ahead of me, and mustn't stand idling."

I sat a while longer, talking with Mrs. M——, and then retired, saying to myself, "Poor woman! Your work is too hard for you. It is wasting your life away. Your slender frame was never made for toil like this."

Passing from the door of my humble neighbor, I crossed the street, and rang at a house of more imposing aspect than hers. A servant showed me into a handsomely furnished parlor, where I waited several minutes for the lady on whom I had called.

"Are you sick, Mrs. B——?" said I, as I took her hand, and looked with concern into my neighbor's pale, troubled face.

"Not sick," she answered, "but worried half out of my life. Sit down, I am glad to see you."

"What has happened to worry you?" I inquired; "any thing more than usual?"

"There's always something more than usual happening in this house," she replied, in a fretful way; "it seems to me that nothing goes right. Just come up-stairs, and I'll show you something."

She arose and I followed her, ascending to the chamber on the next floor. It had been newly papered, I saw at a glance.

"Now just look at that border!" she said, pointing upward. "Isn't it horrid? It spoils the whole effect of the room. The piece I chose was lovely. What possessed the man to substitute this, is more than I can tell. He came while I was out, and the room was finished when I returned."

I looked at the border, but made no remark.

"Did you ever see any thing so outlandish?" said Mrs. B——, with an expression of disgust on her face.

I suppose it must be set down to my want of taste in things ornamental, but I could not see in what the border was out of keeping with the style of paper. To me it was very neat and appropriate.

"I can never endure it!" ejaculated Mrs. B——, in a disturbed manner. "Never! The man must take it off. It will be a constant eyesore. And just look how poorly he has matched the pattern under that window."

I looked to the place indicated, but my eyes failed to see the defect. On going nearer, however, I noticed a very slight deviation from the right line of contact between two parts of a grape-leaf. My wonder was, how Mrs. B—— had managed to discover the fact. I am sure it would not have been revealed to one pair of eyes in a hundred.

"There's no trusting anybody to do things right," continued Mrs. B——, in a nervous, complaining way. "As if I hadn't enough to worry me already, this must be added! It has set my head to aching as if it would burst."

"How is little Freddy?" I asked, wishing

to turn her thoughts to something more pleasant.

"I am dreadfully worried about him," she
replied—the troubled aspect of her face taking on a new and more painful character.

"Is he sick ?"

"No, he's not just sick; but I expect he
will be. Only to think of it! I sent the
nurse out with him yesterday to get the fresh
air. She was gone a long time; so long, that
I got very uneasy. I questioned her closely,
when she came back; and, would you believe it?—the creature owned to having been
to see one of her Irish friends somewhere in
the lower part of the town! Of course, it was
in some low, dirty hovel, and among filthy,
diseased children. Who knows but my dear
little Freddy has been exposed to the infec-
tion of small-pox or scarlet fever? Why, I
hardly slept an hour at a time all night, thinking about it. He looked heavy and drooping
this morning, and I sent for the doctor."

"What did he say ?" I asked.

"Oh!" she replied, "doctors never give

you any satisfaction. He made light of the matter, of course. But I understand the meaning of that. He didn't wish to alarm me. I shan't have a moment's peace of mind for a week to come."

I suggested that it was only conjecture as to the child's having been exposed to disease; and that she might be fretting herself to no purpose. This, instead of allaying, seemed to increase her disturbance of mind. So I tried a new subject; seizing upon the first one that presented itself. I knew that she had obtained, a few weeks before, a first-rate cook.

"Lucy still gives satisfaction?"

"Yes," she replied, "but I don't expect her to stay."

"Why not?"

"Oh! girls that are worth having never stay long. She's the best cook I ever had; but I expect, every day, to receive notice that she is going to leave us."

I smiled, in spite of the solemn face that looked into mine.

"I am afraid you take trouble on interest, Mrs. B——. 'Sufficient unto the day is the evil thereof.' Enjoy your good cook while you have her. It will be time enough to be uncomfortable when she leaves; and that may not be in the next five years."

"It's easy enough to talk," replied Mrs. B——, a little impatiently; "but if you'd passed through what I have—"

She stopped suddenly, bent her head toward the door, and listened.

"That's Freddy now!"

I heard the child's waking cry.

"Come with me to the nursery," said Mrs. B——, moving toward the door. I followed. The child had just wakened from a long nap, and was fretting as we often see children when aroused from sleep.

"Just look how red his face is!" exclaimed Mrs. B——; "are you sick, darling?" and she gathered him up in her arms. "Just feel his hand; it is burning with fever."

I took the soft little hand in mine, and held it for a few moments, to mark the degree of heat.   To me, there was nothing beyond the warmth of vigorous health.

"There's no fever here, Mrs. B——," said I, confidently.

"Yes, there is," she replied.   "He's got a high fever.   Is your throat sore, darling?"

Freddy put his hand to his neck and swallowed once or twice.

"Does it hurt, love?"

The child nodded his head in assent.

The face of Mrs. B—— grew suddenly pale as ashes.

"There, I knew it! I knew it! He's getting the scarlet fever.   Oh, dear!" and she laid her face down among her child's sunny curls, and sobbed wildly.

"Pray, don't distress youself, Mrs. B——, Freddy is not sick," I urged.   But my words had no effect upon her.   She sobbed on for some minutes, until agitation exhausted itself.

"Will you ring the bell?" she asked, at length, looking at me with a sad, tearful face.

I pulled the bell-rope, and the nurse came in almost immediately.

"You must go for the doctor," said Mrs. B——. "Freddy is sick. He's getting the scarlet fever."

The girl looked frightened, and went hurriedly from the room.

"Don't be alarmed, my dear Mrs. B——," said I, trying to reassure her; "I am certain Freddy is not sick. Why, his hand is no hotter than mine. As I took his hand again, my own came in contact with hers. It was cold as marble. No wonder the babe's soft, warm flesh was burning to her touch.

"Feel my hand," I said, "mine and Freddy's together, and see which is hottest."

"You have fever," she replied.

"No," said I, "your hand is icy cold; it has deceived you. Freddy has no fever."

By the time the doctor arrived, Freddy was playing about the floor as lively as a cricket, and I had succeeded in convincing Mrs. B—— that he was in no imminent danger. But the mother was in most need of medical

14

attention. Her nervous fears had so exhausted her, that she was unable to hold her head up. She was lying on the sofa when thé doctor came, her face of a deathly hue. He scolded her soundly, saying that she would kill herself if she went on in this way ; madé a prescription for her, without noticing, except casually, the child, and went off. As my presence could hardly be agreeable to either party, I retired also, pondering the case in my philosophical way.

"Worry is worse than work," said I, "without any doubt. . If Mrs. B—— keeps on after this fashion, she'll shuffle off her mortal coil ín less time than poor Mrs. M——."

On the next morning, I saw Mrs. M——, bright and early, on her way to a neighbor's house, where the day was to be spent at the ironing-table ; her children remaining at home in the care of their oldest sister—herself but a child.

"How's Mrs. B—— ?" I asked of the nurse, whom I saw standing at her door, about ten o'clock, with Freddy in her arms.

The child looked the very picture of health.

"Sick in bed, ma'am," she replied.

"Indeed, what ails her?" I asked.

"Oh! she worried herself sick yesterday, ma'am, about Freddy. And it wasn't a bit of use. Nothing at all was the matter with him, dear little fellow!"

I passed on, saying to myself—"Yes, Mrs. M—— was right; worry kills quicker than work. If Mrs. B—— keeps on as fast as she is now going, she'll get to the end of her journey long before her hard-toiling neighbor."

X.

TELL YOUR WIFE.

"TELL my wife!" said Aaron Little, speaking aloud, yet to himself, in a half amused, half troubled way. "Tell my wife, indeed! Much good that will do! What does she know about business, and money-matters, and the tricks of trade? No, no; there's no hope there."

And Aaron Little sat musing, with a perplexed countenance. He held a newspaper in his hand, and his eyes had just been lingering over a paragraph, in which the writer suggested to business men in trouble, the propriety of consulting their wives:

"Talk to them freely about your affairs," it said. "Let them understand exactly your condition. Tell them of your difficulties, of your embarrassments, and of your plans for extricating yourselves from the entanglements in which you are involved. My word for it, you will get help in nine cases out of ten. Women have quick perceptions. They reach conclusions by a nearer way than reasoning, and get at the solution of a difficult question, long before your slow moving thoughts bring you near enough for accurate observation. Tell your wives, then, men in trouble, all about your affairs! Keep nothing back. The better they understand the matter, the clearer will be their perceptions."

"All a very fine theory," said Aaron Little, tossing the newspaper from him and leaning back in his chair. "But it won't do in my case. Tell Betsy! Yes, I'd like to see myself doing it. A man must be hard pushed indeed, when he goes home to consult his wife on business affairs."

And so Aaron Little dismissed the subject. He was in considerable doubt and perplexity of mind. Things had not gone well with him for a year past. Dull business and bad debts had left his affairs in rather an unpromising condition. He could not see his way clear for the future. Taking trade as it had been for the past six months, he could not imagine how, with the resources at his command, his maturing payments were to be made.

"I must get more capital," he said to himself. "That is plain. And with more capital, must come in a partner. I don't like partnerships. It is so difficult for two men to work together harmoniously. Then you may get entangled with a rogue. It's a risky business. But I see no other way out of this trouble. My own capital is too light for the business I am doing; and as a measure of safety more must be brought in. Lawrence is anxious to join me, and says that he can command ten thousand dollars. I don't like him in all respects; he's a little too fond of pleasure. But I want his money more than his aid in the business. He might remain a silent partner if he chose. I'll call and see him this very night, and have a little talk on the subject. If he can bring in ten thousand dollars, I think that will settle the matter."

With this conclusion in his mind, Aaron Little returned home, after closing his store for the day. Tea being over, he made preparation for going out, with the intention of calling upon Mr. Lawrence. As he reached his hand for his great-coat, a voice seemed to say to him:

"Tell your wife. Talk to her about it."

But he rejected the thought instantly, and commenced drawing on his coat.

"Where are you going, Aaron?" asked Mrs. Little, coming forth from the dining room.

"Out, for a little while," he replied. "I'll be back in half an hour or so."

"Out where?"

"Tell her, Aaron. Tell her all about it," said the voice, speaking in his mind.

"Nonsense! She don't understand any thing about business. She can't help me." He answered, firmly.

"Tell your wife!" The words were in his mind, and would keep repeating themselves.

"Can't you say where you're going, Aaron?
Why do you make a mystery of it?"

"Oh, it's only on a matter of business.
I'm going to see Mr. Lawrence."

"Edward Lawrence!"

"Yes."

"Tell your wife!" The words seemed almost as if uttered aloud in his ears.

"What are you going to see him about?"

"Tell her!"

Mr. Little stood irresolute. What good
would telling her do?

"What's the matter, Aaron? You've
been dull for some time past. Nothing going
wrong with you, I hope!" And his wife
laid her hand upon his arm, and leaned towards him in a kind way.

"Nothing very wrong," he answered in an
evasive manner. "Business has been dull
this season."

"Has it? I'm sorry. Why didn't you tell
me?"

"What good would that have done?"

"It might have done a great deal of good.

When a man's business is dull, his wife should look to the household expenses; but if she knows nothing about it, she may go on in a way that is really extravagant under the circumstances. I think that men ought always to tell their wives, when any thing is going wrong."

"You do?"

"Certainly I do. What better reason can you want than the one I have given? If she knows that the income is reduced, as a prudent wife, she will endeavor to reduce the expenses. Hadn't you better take off your coat, and sit down and talk with me a little, before you go to see Mr. Lawrence?"

"Mr. Little permitted his wife to draw off his overcoat, which she took into the passage and replaced on the hat-rack. Then returning into the parlor, she said:

"Now, Aaron, talk to me as freely as you choose. Don't keep any thing back. Whatever the trouble is, let me know it to the full extent."

"Oh, there's no very great trouble yet. I

am only afraid of trouble. I see it coming, and wish to keep out of its way, Betsy."

"That's wise and prudent," said his wife. "Now tell me why you are going to see Mr. Lawrence."

Mr. Little let his eyes fall to the floor, and sat for some moments in silence. Then looking up, he said:

"The truth is, Betsy, I must have more capital in my business. There will be no getting on without it. Now Mr. Lawrence can command, or at least says he can command, ten thousand dollars. I think he would like to join me. He has said as much two or three times."

"And you were going to see him on that business?"

"I was."

"Don't do it," said Mrs. Little, emphatically.

"Why not?" asked Aaron.

"Because he isn't the man for you—not if he had twenty thousand dollars."

"Because is no reason," replied Aaron Little.

"The extravagance of his wife is," was answered, firmly.

"What do you know about her?"

"Only what I have seen. I've called on her two or three times, and have noticed the style in which her house is furnished. It is arrayed in palace attire, compared with ours. And as for dress, it would take the interest of a little fortune to pay her milliner's and mantua-maker's bills. No, no, Aaron; Mr. Lawrence isn't your man, depend on it. He'd use up the ten thousand dollars in less than two years."

"Well, Betsy, that's pretty clear talk," said Mr. Little, taking a long breath. "I'm rather afraid, after what you say, that Mr. Lawrence is not my man. But what am I to do?" and his voice fell into a troubled tone. "I must have more capital; or——" Mr. Little paused.

"Or what?" His wife looked at him steadily, and without any sign of weak anxiety.

"Or I may become bankrupt."

"I'm sorry to hear you say that, Aaron,"

and Mrs. Little's voice trembled perceptibly. "But I'm glad you've told me. The new parlor carpet, of course, I shall not order."

"Oh, as to that, the amount it will cost can make no great difference," said Mr. Little. "The parlor does look shabby; and I know you've set your heart on a new carpet."

"Indeed, and it *will* make a difference, then," replied the little woman in her decided way. "The last feather breaks the camel's back. Aaron Little shall never fail because of his wife's extravagance. I wouldn't have a new carpet now if it were offered to me at half price."

"You are a brave, true woman, Betsy," said Aaron, kissing his wife, in the glow of a new-born feeling of admiration.

"I hope that I shall ever be a true, brave wife," returned Mrs. Little; "willing always to help my husband, either in saving or in earning, as the case may be. But let us talk more about your affairs; let me see the trouble nearer. Must you have ten thousand dollars right away?"

"Oh, no, no; it's not so bad as that. I was only looking ahead, and seeking to provide the means for approaching payments. I don't want a partner, as far as the business itself is concerned. I don't like partnerships; they are almost always accompanied with annoyances or danger. It was the money I was after; not the man."

"The money would come dearly at the price of the man, if you took Mr. Lawrence for a partner. At least, that is my opinion. But I am glad to hear you say, Aaron, that you are in no immediate danger. May not the storm be weathered by reefing sail, as the sailors say?"

"By reducing expenses?"

"Yes."

Mr. Little shook his head.

"Don't say no too quickly," replied his wife. "Let us go over the whole matter at home and at the store. Suppose two or three thousand dollars were saved in the year. What difference would that make?"

"Oh, if that were possible, which it is not,

it would make a vast difference in the long run; but would hardly meet the difficulties that are approaching."

"Suppose you had a thousand dollars within the next two months, beyond what your business will give?"

"That sum would make all safe for the two months. But where is the thousand dollars to come from, Betsy?"

"Desperate diseases require desperate remedies," replied the brave little woman, in a resolute way. "I'm not afraid of the red flag."

"What do you mean by the red flag?"

"Let us sell off our furniture at auction, and put the money in your business. It won't bring less than a thousand dollars; and it may bring two. My piano alone is worth three hundred and fifty. We can board for a year or two; and when you get all right again, return to housekeeping."

"We won't try that yet, Betsy," said Mr. Little.

"But something must be done. The disease is threatening, and my first prescription will arrest its violence. I have something more to propose. It comes into my mind this instant; after breaking up, we will go to mother's. You know she never wanted us to leave there. It won't cost us much over half what it does now, taking rent into the account. We will pay sister Annie something to take the care of little Eddie and Lizzie through the day, and I will go into your store as chief clerk."

"Betsy! you're crazy!"

"Not a bit of it, Aaron; but a sensible woman, as you will find before you're a year older, if you'll let me have my way. I don't like that Hobson, and never did, as you know. I do'nt believe he's a fair man. Let me take his place, and you will make a clear saving of fifteen hundred dollars a year; and, may-be, of as much more."

"I can't think of it, Betsy. Let us wait awhile."

"You must think of it, and we won't wait awhile," replied the resolute wife. "What

is right to be done is best done quickly. Is
there not safety in my plan?"

"Yes, I think there is; but——"

"Then let us adopt it at once and throw all
buts overboard, or," and she looked at him a little mischievously, "perhaps you would rather
have some talk with Mr. Lawrence, first?"

"Hang Mr. Lawrence!" ejaculated Aaron
Little.

"Very well; there being no help in Mr.
Lawrence, we will go to work to help ourselves. Self-help, I've heard it said, is always the best help, and most to be depended
on. We may know ourselves and trust ourselves; and that is a great deal more than we
can say about other people. When shall we
have the sale?"

"Not so fast, Betsy, not so fast. I haven't
agreed to the sale yet. That would be to
make a certain loss. Furniture sold at auction never realizes above half its cost."

"It would be a certain gain, Aaron, if it
saved you from bankruptcy, with which, as I
understand it, you are threatened."

"I think," said Aaron, "we may get on without that. I like the idea of your coming into my store and taking Hobson's place. All the money from retail sales passes through his hands, and he has it in his power, if not honest, to rob me seriously. I've not felt altogether easy in regard to him of late. Why, I can hardly tell. I've seen nothing wrong. But if you take his place, fifteen hundred dollars will be saved certainly."

"But if I have my house to keep," Mrs. Little answered to this, "how can I help you at the store? The first thing in order is to get the house off of my hands."

"Don't you think that Annie could be induced to come and live with us for a few months until we try this new experiment?"

"But the money, Aaron; the money this furniture would bring! That's what I'm looking after. You want money now."

"Very true."

"Then let us hang out the red flag. Halfway measures may only ruin every thing. I know that mother will not let Annie leave

home ; so it's no use to think of it.   The red
flag, Aaron—the red flag ! Depend upon it,
that's the first right thing to be done.   A
thousand or fifteen hundred dollars in hand
will make you feel like another person—give
you courage, confidence, and energy."

"You may be right, Betsy; but I can't
bear the thought of running out that red flag,
of which you talk so lightly."

"Shall I say coward? Are you afraid to
do what common prudence tells you is
right ?"

"I *was* afraid, Betsy; but am no longer
faint-hearted.   With such a brave little wife
as you, to stand by my side, I need not fear
the world !"

In a week from that day, the red flag was
hung out.   When the auctioneer made up his
accounts, he had in hand a little over eighteen
hundred dollars, for which a check was filled
out to the order of Aaron Little.   It came
into his hands just at the right moment, and
made him feel, to use his own words, "as
easy as an old shoe."   One week later, Mrs.

Betsy Little took the place of Mr. Hobson, as chief manager and cash-receiver, in her husband's store. There were some few signs of rebellion among the clerks and shop-girls at the beginning; but Mrs. Betsy had a quick, steady eye, and a self-reliant manner that caused her presence felt, and soon made every thing subservient to her will. It was a remarkable fact, that at the close of the first week of her administration of affairs, the cash receipts were over a hundred and fifty dollars in excess of the receipts of any week within the previous three months.

"Have we done more business than usual this week?" she asked of one clerk and another; and the uniform answer was, "No."

"Then," said the lady to herself, "there's been foul play here. No wonder my husband was in trouble."

At the end of the next week, the sales came up to the same average, and at the end of the third week were two hundred dollars better than before Mrs. Little undertook to manage the retail department. Whether there had been "foul play" or not, Aaron Little could never fully determine; but he was in no doubt as to one thing, and that was the easy condition of the money market, after the lapse of half a year.

For four or five months previous to Mrs. Little's administration of affairs, he was on the street for nearly half his time, during business hours, engaged in the work of money-raising; now his regular receipts had got in advance of his payments; so that his balance on the morning of each day was usually in excess of the notes to be lifted. Of course, he could give more attention to business; and, of course, business increased and grew more profitable under the improved system. By the end of the year, to use his own words, he was "all right." Not so a neighbor of his, who, to get more capital, had taken Mr. Lawrence as a partner. Instead of bringing in ten thousand dollars, that "capitalist" was only able to put down three thousand; and before the end of the year he had drawn out six or seven thousand, and had given notes of the firm for as much more in payment of old obligations. A failure of the house followed as an inevitable result.

When the fact of the failure, and the cause which led to it, became known to Mr. Little, he remarked, with a shrug:

"I'm sorry for B——, but he should have told his wife."

"Of what?" asked the person to whom he addressed the remark.

"Of his want of more capital, and intention to make a partner of Lawrence."

"What good would that have done?"

"It might have saved him from ruin, as it did me."

"You are mysterious, Little."

"Am I? Well, in plain words: a year ago I was hard up for money in my business, and thought of taking in Lawrence. I told my wife about it. She said, 'Don't do it.' And I didn't; for her 'Don't do it' was followed by suggestions as to his wife's extravagance that opened my eyes a little. I told her, at the same time, of my embarrassments, and she set her bright little head to work, and showed me the way to work out of them. Before this I always had a poor opinion of woman's wit in matters of business; but now I say to every man in trouble—

"'Tell your wife!'"

XI.

UNCLE PHIL.'S REMEDY.

"How's Mary?" asked Uncle Phil. Windham, of his nephew, Harry Lester.

"Not very well," replied the young man, with a shadowed face.

"I'm sorry. What seems to be the matter with her?"

"I'm sure I don't know, Uncle Phil. She has no appetite, and is weak and wretched half her time.'

"What does the doctor say?"

"Nothing satisfactory. It's my opinion that he doesn't know what ails her. The worst of it is, she gets into such low spirits, and cries, sometimes, for half the night."

"That's bad, Harry—very bad."

"I know it is, uncle. Yet what can I do?"

"How are you getting along in your business?" asked Uncle Phil.

"Not so well as I could desire. Hard, wearisome work every day, and yet I seem to make very little progress."

The young man's face took on a troubled aspect. Uncle Phil. had seen that look a great many times before, and now it set him to thinking.

"Did you ever see the person who got along in this world as well as he desired?" asked the old man.

"Oh, as to that, Uncle Phil., my desires do not take a very wide range. But, I would like to see some fruit of my labor."

"You have a comfortable home, Harry, as the fruit of your labor. Isn't that something?"

"Yes. But, I don't seem to get ahead. And that discourages me. I work hard enough, in all conscience."

Uncle Phil. looked at his nephew for some moments, and then said:

"Is that the face you carry home every night, Harry?"

"What face? I don't understand you."

"The dark, discontented face you wear now?"

The eyes of Harry Lester dropped to the ground.

"Because, if it is, I don't wonder Mary is sick."

The shadows passed away, and a smile lit up the young man's countenance.

"Ah, that's better!   That's the true home-face.   Show it to Mary, and, my word for it, she'll find it more potent than medicine."

"You're a little facetious to-day, uncle," said Lester.

"Not I; but in sober earnest.   I don't just know how it is; but I'm afraid that, in going home to Mary at night, you take shadows instead of sunshine.   Now, a woman's heart wants sunshine.   It cannot grow flowers in the dark.   Leave your care and business anxiety inside of your store when the doors are shut at night, and bring home to your wife a cheerful spirit.   Try the virtue of a smiling face, my boy; and, old Uncle Phil.'s word for it, Mary will need no more doctor's stuff."

It was just as the old man had supposed. Harry Lester, like too many other men who permit themselves to get over-anxious in regard to business matters, always brought a clouded face to his home at night. He used to bring light, and smiles, and cheerful words. Then it was different with Mary from what it was now. Her face reflected the light and smiles that beamed from his, and her lips were running over with pleasant talk. Uncle Phil.'s remarks set him to thinking, and he remembered all this. Could it be possible that the withdrawal of sunlight from his countenance had thrown her life into shadow?

"I thought she was more of a woman than that."

More of a woman! Why, is this all you know of a true woman's nature? You should have been wiser in regard to her character before taking the happiness of a wife into your keeping. Love cannot grow and flourish if the sky is forever clouded; and love is a woman's life.

The state of Mary's mind, as well as the

state of her health, were sad enough to lead
her husband to think seriously on any remedy
that might be proposed; and so Uncle Phil.'s
admonition did not pass from his thoughts, as
we have seen from his remark touching the
lack of true womanliness in his wife.

"Try the virtue of a smiling face."

That was easily enough said; but not so
easily done.   How was Harry Lester to smile
when he felt depressed in mind, and anxious
about his business?   He could smile through
the day; smile in the face of his customers;
and without an effort.   Did he think of that?
No; he only thought of the impossibility of
applying Uncle Phil.'s remedy.

"Try the virtue of a smiling face, my
boy!"

He remembered these words as he stood at
his door, and made a pause before entering.
Any thing but a smiling aspect was the one
that sat upon his countenance.

"I will try," he answered, with a kind of
desperate resolution, and, pushing open the
door, entered with a lighter step than usual.

"Oh, is this you, Mary?" he said, in a pleasant way, as his wife, who happened to be crossing from the parlor, met him in the passage. He put on a smile as he spoke, and wonderful to say, a smile came into Mary's pale face.

"How are you, this evening?" he then asked, with a kind interest that was unusual, for, nearly always, his thoughts were not home-guests, but wanderers backward amid the cares of the day, or forward with anxious hopes into the morrow.

"Better than I have felt all day." And something of the old sweetness played about her lips; played there so temptingly that her husband could not repress the inclination he felt to lay upon them a kiss of tender feeling.

Why, it seemed as if a sudden sun-burst had irradiated the countenance of Mrs. Lester. How long was it since a kiss, so full of heart-warmth as that, had been pressed upon her lips? Away back in the past, the time lay so far, that memory was at fault in recalling it.

Better than she had felt all day! If this were really so, and we believe it, the discovery was made at the moment.

"I am glad of it, Mary." And with his arm drawn around her waist—when had it been there before?—they walked back into the sitting-room.

"You look in better spirits, dear?" And Mary's eyes read his face all over with an eager interest she could not hide.

It was on the man's lips to reply that he wasn't aware of any cause why he should feel in better spirits. Despondency was such a habit with him, that any other state of mind seemed unusual. Even as the words of this reply came into his mind, his countenance changed. But, remembering Uncle Phil.'s admonition, he checked himself, and forcing back into life the already half-extinguished smile, answered:

"Do I?"

"Yes; in better spirits than I have seen you for a long time. It does me good to see the sunshine in your face again."

"The sunshine in my face again, Mary? Why, has it been absent so long?"

Lester felt surprise, and showed it in his manner.

"Don't let it go out again, dear," said his wife, leaning fondly towards him.

"If it is so pleasant to you, Mary——"

"Pleasant, Harry! It is my life. Oh, if I could see your face wearing the cheerful expression it wore in the beginning of our married life, I would be the happiest woman alive."

Mrs. Lester's voice lost itself in a sob; and her eyes grew dim with tears; but the smile that lit up her wan face, and gave to it an impression of former beauty, remained.

"Business brings its cares and anxieties, Mary; and these will shadow the face sometimes."

"I know it, dear. But, why not leave care and anxious thoughts behind, when the day's business is over? To sit at home in darkness, cannot make you stronger for tomorrow's work. It is enough to be anxious and careful all day. Evening should refresh your mind with cheerfulness."

"True words, Mary; and I will try to profit by them. It does me good to see the sunshine in your face again."

"You can always have it there if you will," she answered.

"I can?"

"Yes; but only reflected sunshine. I am like the moon, and shine by borrowed light. If clouds cover your face, mine must lie in darkness."

That was an evening memorable in after times, as the happiest one they had known for months, if not for years. Mary's aspect changed in an hour so entirely, that she scarcely seemed like the same person. A neighbor who dropped in during the evening, said: "How much better you look, Mrs. Lester! I'm really glad to see it."

"I feel much better than I have felt for a long time," she replied.

Her husband looked and listened in wonder

and self-rebuke. Uncle Phil.'s new remedy was working like a " charm."

"Can it be possible," he said to himself, "that the cause of her low spirits and failing health lies at my door ? Has she been wasting like a plant deprived of sunshine ? I did not dream of this. Women are different from men. I have not comprehended my wife."

In the morning Mrs. Lester looked cheerful, and moved about with a lightness of step to which she had been for months a stranger. There was even warmth in the cheeks that had been colorless so long; a warmth that gave them an appearance of roundness.

" How is Mary, to day ?" asked Uncle Phil., who called at the store of his nephew.

" She's better, I thank you."

" Ah! I'm glad to hear you say so. Did you try my remedy ?" The old man smiled, and Lester smiled back in his face.

" Did you try it ?"

"Yes."

" And it acted right ?"

" Like a charm !"

"I knew it would!" said the old man, gleefully. "I knew it would! Why, you moody fellow! you were killing your wife. Women must have a little sunshine at home, or they will die. And so Mary is better, dear heart! I was sure that was all she wanted. I was sure I had the right remedy."

"If there should be no relapse."

"Relapse! There can be no relapse, un-less you take home a rueful face. Let her see you always cheerful and hopeful, and, my word for it, there will be no going back to low spirits."

"But, Uncle Phil.," said the young man, "how am I always to look cheerful and hope-ful, when my mind is burdened with care? It is requiring of me a great deal more, I am afraid, than I can give."

"Did your worrying all through the even-ing ever help you a particle on the next day, Harry?" asked the old man.

"I don't know that it did; still I couldn't help worrying."

"I know better. You can help worrying,
16

if you will.   You helped it last night, didn't you?"

" Yes."

" And you can help it to-night, and to-morrow night, if you will."

" How?"

"Think of your wife's health and happiness.   That should be motive enough, surely, to cause a little self-denial."

" Self-denial, Uncle Phil.!"

" Yes; for I think you must have a certain enjoyment in these moody states, else you would not indulge them so often.   Your own reason tells you that they are fruitful of great harm.   But a deeper reason why they should cease is, that they involve distrust in Providence.   Harry, you are in the hands of one who knows your wants, and who will see that they are provided for just in the degree that is best for your eternal as well as your earthly good.   No anxious care; no dread of coming disaster; no gloomy distrust or chafing doubt will change the events of to-morrow.   They are to be ministers of good to

you, though not always in the way you have
desired.   Is it not the worst of folly, then, to
sit brooding in darkness because the affairs of
your daily life do not shape themselves according to your short-sighted plannings? You
can help this unhappy brooding over what
cannot be changed, and you must do it."

"I will try," answered the young man.

"You must try, and succeed also.   Let
there be no giving up or going back.   Habit
is second nature.   You have fallen into a bad
habit.   Break it up with a vigorous hand,
and go to work in the formation of a good
habit.   After a while, you will find it as easy
to carry home a pleasant face as you now do
a clouded one.   And think what a wonderful
difference it will make in your home!"

When the day went down, and Lester
turned his steps homeward, he felt the old,
dark states falling like funereal drapery
around him.   There had been nothing in the
day's business of an unusually depressing
character.   It had been a fair day's business,
and he should have been satisfied.   But hav-

ing indulged a morbid way of looking at things so long, his mind had taken on a diseased action, and now there was a troubled weight on his feelings, and a depression of spirits that it seemed impossible to throw off. Thus it was with him when he ascended the steps of his dwelling, and reached out his hand to open the door.

"This will not do," he said, pausing. And he stood still at the unopened door for some moments. "I shall mar every thing."

Then he descended the steps, and passed up the street.

"It will never do in the world to carry this face home to Mary. I must try and find a better one. What a firm grip this fiend of brooding distrust has taken! I must shake him off, and I will!" Thus he talked with himself, as he strode away.

In ten minutes Lester was back again at his own door; and now he turned the key and entered without hesitation. He had shaken off the fiend, and had a smile, a kiss, and a pleasant word for Mary, which gave new life to her pulses, and sent the warm blood in flushes of beauty to her face.

Two applications of Uncle Phil.'s remedy were enough to satisfy Henry Lester of the real cause of his wife's disease; and to assure him that he had only to continue as he had begun to make certain of a speedy cure. He found the remedy good for himself also. His own mind had been diseased as well as the mind of his wife; but now he felt like a new man. Health was flowing through his veins, and giving him a sense of enjoyment to which he had been a stranger for years.

NEW JUVENILE BOOKS,
To be ready early in the coming Fall.

A NEW SERIES BY AUNT FANNY,
Author of "Nightcap," "Mitten," and "Pet Books."

THE POP-GUN STORIES.
In 6 vols. 16mo., beautifully illustrated.

I.—POP-GUNS.
II.—ONE BIG POP-GUN.
III.—ALL SORTS OF POP-GUNS.
IV.—FUNNY POP-GUNS.
V.—GRASSHOPPER POP-GUNS.
VI.—POST-OFFICE POP-GUNS.

Aunt Fanny is one of the most successful writers for children in this country, as is attested by the very wide sale her previous books have had, and we feel sure that the mere announcement of this new series will attract the attention of her host of admirers.

A NEW SERIES BY T. S. ARTHUR,
Author of "Household Library," and "Arthur's Juvenile Library."

HOME STORIES.
3 vols., 16mo., fully illustrated.

LIST OF VOLUMES.

HIDDEN WINGS.
SOWING THE WIND.
SUNSHINE AT HOME.

The name of this Author is a sufficient Guarantee of the excellence of the Series.

ROLLO'S TOUR IN EUROPE.

BY JACOB ABBOTT,

Author of the "Rollo Books;" "Florence Stories," "American Histories," &c., &c.

ORDER OF THE VOLUMES.

ROLLO ON THE ATLANTIC.
ROLLO IN PARIS.
ROLLO IN SWITZERLAND.
ROLLO IN LONDON.
ROLLO ON THE RHINE.
ROLLO IN SCOTLAND.
ROLLO IN GENEVA.
ROLLO IN HOLLAND.
ROLLO IN NAPLES.
ROLLO IN ROME.

Each volume fully illustrated.

Price per vol., 90 cents.

Mr. Abbott is the most successful writer of books for the young in this, or perhaps, any other country. "ROLLO'S TOUR IN EUROPE," is by far the greatest success of any of Mr. Abbott's works.

From the New York Observer.

"Mr. Abbott is known to be a pure, successful and useful writer for the young and old. He is also the most popular Author of juvenile books now living."

PETER PARLEY'S OWN STORY.

From the Personal Narrative of the late SAMUEL G. GOOD-
RICH (Peter Parley).

1 vol. 16mo, illustrated, price $1.25.

CHILDREN'S SAYINGS;
OR, EARLY LIFE AT HOME.

By CAROLINE HADLEY. With Illustrations, by WALTER
CRANE.

1 vol. square 16mo, price 90 cents.

STORIES OF OLD.
OLD TESTAMENT SERIES.

By CAROLINE HADLEY.

1 vol. 12mo, Illustrated, price $1.25.

STORIES OF OLD.
NEW TESTAMENT SERIES.

By CAROLINE HADLEY.

1 vol. 12mo, Illustrated, price $1.25.

ROSE MORTON'S JOURNAL.

A series of volumes containing Rose Morton's Journal for the
several months of the year.

Each volume Illustrated, 18mo, 45 cents.

There are now ready,

ROSE MORTON'S JOURNAL FOR JANUARY.
ROSE MORTON'S JOURNAL FOR FEBRUARY.
ROSE MORTON'S JOURNAL FOR MARCH.
ROSE MORTON'S JOURNAL FOR APRIL.
ROSE MORTON'S JOURNAL FOR MAY.

WALTER'S TOUR IN THE EAST.

A Series of interesting Travels through Egypt, Palestine
Turkey, and Syria. By Rev. D. C. EDDY, D.D.

Each volume beautifully Illustrated from Designs brought
from those countries.

Each volume, 16mo, price 90 cents.

There are now ready:

> Walter in Egypt.
> Walter in Jerusalem.
> Walter in Samaria.
> Walter in Damascus.
> Walter in Constantinople.   (In press.)

From the New York Commercial Advertiser.

"Dr. Eddy is known as the author of 'The Percy Family,' and is a
most pleasing and instructive writer for the young. The present volume
is one of a series of six, describing a visit of a company of young tourists
to the most interesting and sacred spots on the earth. The incidents recited and the facts presented are just such as will captivate while they
instruct intelligent youth, and give even adult minds some correct ideas
of Eastern countries and habits. In the present volume, Walter travels
through Egypt, and his story is told in some two hundred and twenty
pages ; so compactly told, indeed, that not a line could have been omitted
without injury. It is just the book for an intelligent child.

From the Pittsburgh Gazette.

"There are four very appropriate illustrations, representing the scenery
and incidents of travel in Egypt. The volume, moreover, is well written,
handsomely printed at the Riverside press, neatly bound in cloth, and
therefore may be commended as a suitable holiday present,—a book that
will both instruct and interest youthful readers."

From the Buffalo Express.

"This beautiful little volume is the first of a series of six, describing the
visit of a company of young tourists to the most interesting and sacred
spots on the earth. In the one under consideration, a number of incidents
are recited, and facts presented, which will be found not only exceedingly
interesting and instructive to boys and girls, but will give even adult
minds some idea of the romantic East. It is elegantly bound, and illus-

ABBOTT'S AMERICAN HISTORY.

A Series of American Histories for Youth, by Jacob Abbott.

To be completed in Eight Volumes, 18mo, price 1 dollar each
Each volume complete in itself.

Each volume will be illustrated with numerous Maps and En-
gravings, from original designs, by F. O. C. Darley, J. R. Chapin,
G. Perkins, Charles Parsons, H. W. Herrick, E. F. Beaulieu,
H. L. Stephens, and others.

This Series, by the well-known author of the "Rollo
Books," "Rollo's Tour in Europe," "Harper's Series of
European Histories," "The Florence Stories," &c., will
consist of the following volumes:

1. Aboriginal America.

2. Discovery of America.

3. Southern Colonies.

4. The Northern Colonies.

5. Wars of the Colonies.

6. The Revolt of the Colonies.

7. Revolution. (Ready in November.)

8. Washington.

NOTICES OF THE INITIAL VOLUME.

From the Boston Traveller.
"The most excellent publication of the kind ever undertaken."

From the Boston Advertiser.
"The illustrations are well designed and executed."

From the Boston Post.
"One of the most useful of the many good and popular books of which
Mr. Abbott is the author."

From the Philadelphia North American.
"It is indeed a very vivid and comprehensive presentation of the phys-
ical aspect and aboriginal life visible on this continent, before the discovery
by white men."

From the Troy Whig.
"Mr. Abbott's stories have for years been the delight of thousands."

THE ROLLO STORY BOOKS.

By JACOB ABBOTT.

Trouble on the Mountain,	Georgie,
Causey Building,	Rollo in the Woods,
Apple Gathering,	Rollo's Garden,
The Two Wheelbarrows,	The Steeple Trap,
Blueberrying,	Labor Lost,
The Freshet,	Lucy's Visit.

12 vols. 18mo. Cloth. Illustrated. Price, per set, $4.50

THE FLORENCE STORIES.

By JACOB ABBOTT.

Vol. 1.—Florence and John. 18mo. Cloth. Illustrated.
Vol. 2.—Grimkie. 18mo. Cloth. Illustrated.
Vol. 3.—The Isle of Wight. 18mo. Cloth. Illustrated.
Vol. 4.—The Orkney Islands. 18mo. Cloth. Illustrated.
Vol. 5.—The English Channel. 18mo. Cloth. Illustrated.
Vol. 6.—Florence's Return. 18mo. Cloth. Illustrated.

Price of each volume $1.00.

From the Boston Journal.

"Mr. Abbott is always an entertaining writer for the young, and this story seems to us to contain more that is really suggestive and instructive than other of his recent productions. Florence and John are children who pursue their studies at home, under the care of their mother, and in the progress of the tale many useful hints are given in regard to home instruction. The main educational idea which runs through all Mr. Abbott's works, that of developing the capacities of children so as to make them self-reliant, is conspicuous in this."

From the New York Observer.

"Mr. Abbott is known to be a pure, successful and useful writer for the young and old. He is also the most popular author of juvenile books now living."

From the Boston Traveller.

"No writer of children's books, not even the renowned Peter Parley has ever been so successful as Abbott."

THE BRIGHTHOPE SERIES.

By J. T. TROWBRIDGE.

The Old Battle Ground,
Father Brighthope,
Hearts and Faces.

Iron Thorpe,
Burr Cliff.

5 vols. 18mo, in cloth, gilt back, uniform. Price 75 cts. each.

From the Boston Transcript.

" Mr. Trowbridge has never written anything that was not popular, and each new work has added to his fame. He has a wonderful faculty as a portrayer of New England characteristics, and New England scenes."

From the Salem Register.

" Mr. Trowbridge will find many welcomers to the field of authorship as often as he chooses to enter it, and to leave as pleasant a record behind him as the story of "Father Brighthope." The "Old Battle Ground" is worthy of his reputation as one of the very best portrayers of New England character and describers of New England scenes."

THE GELDART SERIES.

By Mrs. THOMAS GELDART.

6 vols. 16mo. Illustrated by JOHN GILBERT.
Price of each 60 cents.

Daily Thoughts for a Child,
Truth is Everything,
Sunday Morning Thoughts,

Sunday Evening Thoughts,
Emilie the Peacemaker.
Stories of Scotland.

From the Boston Register.

" These charming volumes are the much admired Geldart Series of books for the young, which have established a very enviable reputation in England for their wholesome moral tendency. They are beautifully printed 16mo volumes, with gilt backs, and are sold at 50 cents each. There are five volumes in the series, and they will form a very choice addition to a youth's library."

From the Worcester Palladium.

" What children read they often long retain; therefore it is desirable that their books should be of a high moral tone. In this respect Mrs. Geldart has few equals as an author, and we hope that her works will be found in every child's library."

FORTY YEARS' EXPERIENCE IN SUNDAY-SCHOOLS.

BY STEPHEN H. TYNG, D.D.,

Rector of St. George's Church, New York.

1 neat 16mo vol., price $1 00.

From the Boston Gazette.

"As a matter of course, the volume is in a measure autobiographical, which would alone secure general attention to it."

From the Southern Churchman.

"No one is entitled to speak about Sunday-tchools with more authority than Dr. Tyng, and no one can read this volume without obtaining most valuable hints for the management of a Sunday-school."

From the Boston Courier.

"This little work of a distinguished divine will doubtless prove of great service to superintendents and teachers of Sunday-schools."

From the Troy Times.

"In a literary point of view, they are marked by all the excellencies for which the reverend author is noted; while the amount of real, useful knowledge they convey in a brief and practical form, upon a subject the importance of which is little understood, is really surprising."

From the N. Y. Intelligencer.

"Few pastors have been favored with so large a measure of experience and success in the work of Sabbath-school instruction as the venerable pastor of St. George's Church. As the present volume contains the results of the author's long experience, it will be a welcome addition to our Sabbath-school literature."

From the N. Y. Independent.

"Every Sabbath-school teacher should read it; every pastor might profit by it."

From the N. Y. Observer.

"This will be a very welcome volume to Sunday-school teachers, and to all who are interested in Sunday-schools. It embodies the experience and the counsels of one who, by his deep interest in the cause, and by a personal devotion to the work, even in its details, and by a success which has been rarely if ever equaled, is qualified to speak with great profit upon the important subject. We have often made mention of the school at St. George's church, as perhaps the largest in the country, and as exhibiting results, not only in the chief end of Sabbath-school instruction, but in the great work of Christian benevolence and Christian activity, which are delightful to contemplate. In these pages the author imparts in a measure, the secret of his success. We are sure that the volume has a great mission to accomplish for good."

THE OAKLAND STORIES.

By George B. Taylor.

Vol. 1.—Kenny. 18mo. Cloth. Illustrated.
Vol. 2.—Cousin Guy. 18mo. Cloth. Illustrated.
Vol. 3.—Claiborne. 18mo. Cloth. Illustrated.

Price of each volume 90 cents.

From the Troy Whig.

"The writer, although by no means an imitator of Jacob Abbott, shows a good deal of talent in the same field."

From the Boston Journal.

"While in general this story resembles Mr. Abbott's, it is superior to some of that author's later works. It is marked by his best characteristics—the easy, natural dialogue, wholesome, moral and religious tone, and simple explanatory style, without being tiresome in repetition. It describes home scenes and suggests home amusements."

THE ROLLO BOOKS.

By Jacob Abbott.

Rollo Learning to Talk,	Rollo's Museum,
Rollo Learning to Read,	Rollo's Travels,
Rollo at Work,	Rollo's Correspondence,
Rollo at Play,	Rollo's Philosophy, Water,
Rollo at School,	Rollo's Philosophy, Air,
Rollo's Vacation,	Rollo's Philosophy, Fire,
Rollo's Experiments,	Rollo's Philosophy, Sky.

14 vols. Illustrated, uniform style. 16mo. Cloth, each 80 cents,

14 vols., uniform style. 18mo., cheap edition "   each 60 cents

HISTORY OF ENGLAND.

By Mrs. THOMAS GELDART,

Author of "Daily Thoughts for a Child," "Stories of Scotland," &c.
With Twenty Illustrations, by J. R. Chapin, and others.
1 vol., 16mo.   Price 90 cents.

From the Detroit Advertiser.

" The work has been executed with rare taste and judgment, and contains all the most important events in the history of England, and all that it is really important for ordinary readers to know."

From the Philadelphia North American.

"Much of the information is quite curious, and drawn from recondite sources."

From the Baltimore Patriot.

"Precisely suited to the rising generation."

From the Boston Journal.

" This work exactly realizes our idea of what a juvenile history should be. It is simple and direct, without degrading the dignity of history; interesting, without converting it into a romance, and above all draws such pictures of dress and manners in the olden time, that instead of a list of hard names, living characters, eating, drinking, and sleeping like ourselves, walk before the mind's eye of the youthful readers. This work does for juveniles what Charles Knight's Popular History is doing for mature readers."

From the Philadelphia City Item.

"We have read the volume, and have pleasure in commending it to public perusal. It is a work for old or young, and it is so full of interest that no one will lay it down until its details have been mastered."

From the Church Journal.

" A very pleasant, easy, readable book is Mrs. Geldart's Popular History of England. She has had long practice in writing for children, and it is such practice as makes perfect."

From the Philadelphia Christian Instructor.

" We know of no History of England so well adapted to prove an attractive and instructive reading-book for young persons as the one before us. The style is very simple, but, at the same time, chaste and elevated; and, what is very important, the book abounds with practical lessons for the young. Although specially designed for this class, it may be read with interest and profit by all persons."

From the New York News.

" British, Danish, and Saxon England, from the conquest of Cæsar to that of William the Norman, is described in this book with a picturesqueness and vigor which make it most fascinating. Designed for the young it has charms for readers of every class and age. The engravings are excellent, and give many drawings of arms, utensils, and implements of the ancient inhabitants of England. It is rather a picture than a history, although historical characters are introduced to give life and interest to the description."

F150-C